T0171562

WILLA VERBANIC

The Unconventional Lady

iUniverse, Inc.
Bloomington

This is a work of fiction. All of the characters, names, incidents, organizations, and dialogue in this novel are either the products of the author's imagination or are used fictitiously.

iUniverse books may be ordered through booksellers or by contacting:

iUniverse
1663 Liberty Drive
Bloomington, IN 47403
www.iuniverse.com
1-800-Authors (1-800-288-4677)

Because of the dynamic nature of the Internet, any Web addresses or links contained in this book may have changed since publication and may no longer be valid. The views expressed in this work are solely those of the author and do not necessarily reflect the views of the publisher, and the publisher hereby disclaims any responsibility for them.

Any people depicted in stock imagery provided by Thinkstock are models, and such images are being used for illustrative purposes only.

Certain stock imagery © Thinkstock.

ISBN: 978-1-4502-8762-3 (sc)
ISBN: 978-1-4502-8763-0 (ebook)

Printed in the United States of America

iUniverse rev. date: 01/31/2011

Chapter 1

As the elevator approached the eighteenth floor, Judy closed her eyes and took several deep breaths. She couldn't believe she was here to be interview for a job in South America. Receiving the call yesterday to come in for an interview surprised her. She was being considered for a position with an international builder.

She had applied on several occasions for work overseas but they had always sent letters saying the position was filled or they no longer needed anyone, but she felt they really meant, we don't want a woman.

Although quite young, Judy was an acclaimed Architect as well as a civil engineer, and had been working with a well-known firm for the past few years. Although she received excellent pay and was well liked, a month ago she decided she wanted to try something more exciting. This job in South America for Hardell International Builders was one she really coveted. There was to be an energy plant, housing and little else was mentioned in the advertisement except it would last about one year.

Judy had worked hard from the day she got out of college to get where she was. She was ambitious, hard working and loved what she did. It was something she had chose before she ever started high school. Her Mothers family was all in construction and at an early age she was fascinated with her grandfather's work and many times was allowed to go on construction sites with him. Although her Father would have preferred her to follow in his footsteps as a pilot, he supported and helped her accomplish her dream. It had not been easy. Judy was an above average student and was always ahead of her friends in classes but always behind in driving, dating and other things. She was in college by the time she was seventeen. Her teachers tried to discourage her choice of profession because most of the classes she chose, even in high school, were all-male students and in college, many times she was the only female in the class.

As the elevator door slid open and Judy stepped off, she took a few deep breaths, stretched to her full height of five foot five inches before going through the door that indicated Hardell International Builders.

Judy was twenty-eight and had her license for several years, her youthful appearance conflicted with her years of experience. She had landed a good job right out of college and had never looked back.

Her Dad has encouraged her to learn to fly and she did, but it did not have the "burning sensation" in it for her. She had learned to fly and enjoyed flying with her Dad and she kept her Small Plane Pilot license active. When she was home she enjoyed flying with her Dad but it was not something she wanted to do on a daily basis.

Chapter 2

Judy had chose a gray wool suit with a green blouse for her interview. The blouse matched her green almond shaped eyes, which were accented by long lushly curled lashes. Her hair was what she called Strawberry Blond, but everyone else insisted on calling her "Red". It was conservatively styled to flatter her light delicate features and her soft pale complexion, which was too sensitive to sun and wind.

The heels of her black pumps sunk into the plush carpet as she approached the reception desk. An attractive brunette in her early twenties smiled as Judy introduced herself and presented the letter for interviewing. The woman took the letter and said, "Mr. Hardell is expecting you, please follow me."

They walked down the hall, stopping at a door with the name "Stewart Hardell" on it. The receptionist knocked, and as they entered she gave Judy a little wink and smiled as she whispered, " Good luck."

As she handed the letter across the desk to a man of about fifty, she said, "Mr. Hardell, this is Judy Winston".

Judy reached out her hand to the man addressed as Mr. Hardell, as he stood up to shake her hand, she could see he was evaluating everything about her. This was no ordinary interview by a personnel manager; "Mr. Hardell International" himself was scrutinizing her.

He motioned for Judy to sit down, "You appear much younger and more…. delicate than I expected." He hesitated before saying delicate and as he did, Judy's eyes shot up, she looked him straight in the eyes, and tried not to show the anger she felt at the remark.

She replied in as calm a voice as she could, "Mr. Hardell, as an Architect and engineer, I can be hard and persistent when needed. As a woman I can be sensitive and understanding, however I learned very early on to keep the two separated. I can be very difficult opponent in negotiations I assure you. I know my job."

He smiled, "That I am well aware of Miss Winston, we lost a very large project to "Girco" while you were working for them and it was because of your efficient work. However, you will have to admit you will be in a completely different element here. I only mentioned your delicacy because of the rough terrain and weather. I realize you have had some, shall we say, difficult assignments for short periods, however, you are aware, this could be up to a year you will be in South America."

"Yes Mr. Hardell, I realize that, and I am sure I can cope with those factors. I am small, but I have always kept fit with exercise and sports, I think the only problem I will have is protecting my skin from the severe heat and sun. I rarely tan, my skin may be delicate but I assure you I am not."

"Well, we seem to have cleared that up quite well Miss Winston. What about personal or family ties that might cause complications. Are they're any?"

Judy knew now why this man was interviewing her. It was his company and this was an unusual position for a woman in the field for a long period. He wanted to make the final decision himself. She had passed his professional requirements, he same as told her that, but he was not sure she could handle a year with all men and rough living conditions for that period of time. Realizing this, Judy relaxed a little and decided if she was going to land this job, she would have to be very open and completely honest so he could judge her personally.

Before answering his questions, she shifted in her seat, relaxing the tension in her body to get more comfortable. This was going to take a while. They talked for almost an hour before he started telling her a few things about the project and what she would be required to do before she left the United State

Chapter 3

She would have a good physical; shots, current passport and her pilot license would have to be updated. There was six weeks to get everything in order. Starting Monday, she would report to the airfield first thing to be tested and checked out on several planes. They wanted her familiar with any she might be flying while in South America. Judy gave a little silent thank you to her Father for her intensive training in flying. In the afternoon she would come to the office for briefings on her job assignment and whatever other planning was necessary.

A list of clothing, supplies and necessary equipment was discussed. Mr. Hardell was showing her some pictured of the job side when it occurred to Judy she had the job. She couldn't believe it was true. He was still talking and she tried to concentrate on what he was saying.

"The man in charge is Benjamin Roads. He is a good man and will appear hard at first, but he will come around after the first shock of us sending a woman down. The second in charge is Michael Downs. Mike is a fun loving, easygoing sort. Both men are excellent engineers and if she had any problems Judy was assured she could depend on them. Don't try to be a loaner. When in isolated areas you depend on each other, so it is imperative you cooperate and get along."

"Along with the two engineers already on the job, there is a construction supervisor and a few construction foreman, the main labor force is local people. The construction supervisor is married as well as two other men, so there are three women from home but none are employees. Ben and Mike have been with the company several years and neither of them is married. There are others as well, but the main work force as I said is local workers."

"You will be provided with living quarters. Your main assignment is to design and oversee the construction of housing and an energy plant for workers that will be running the electrical plant and working the mine. The area is growing and the Brazilian government is concerned about protecting their rain forest."

Hardell International had acquired the contract to design and to build the plant as well as housing for the work force. The Brazilian government will watch closely to make sure we do what is best for their country.

The concern for the environment and protection of the rain forest was the reason Mr. Hardell was interested in Judy. It was because of her expertise that she was selected over all the other applicants, he informed her.

She would design small, two and three bedroom homes, larger ones with four and five bedrooms, and a Guest House with twelve to fifteen rooms to rent out to visiting friends and relatives. Another reason Judy was favored over all the other applicants was the need for a trash to energy plant. She had been instrumental in building one in Canada last year and Mr. Hardell knew she was the designer.

Ben and Mike would decide the best locations for the plant and housing, then access roads would be put in accordingly. There also would be a representative from the Brazilian Government to meet with them on the planning and construction.

After over two hours with Mr. Hardell, Judy was taken to meet some of the staff. Mr. Gray was her link to everything. He was the home office representative in charge of this project. She would report to him starting Monday and he would help her prepare for her assignment. He told her what clothing she would need and scheduled her with a flight instructor starting on Monday. The fact that she had her pilot license was an asset, since it was over eight hundred miles into where they would be working.

Chapter 4

The next few weeks went fast for Judy. She was at the airfield by seven, every day and at night she concentrated on her list of clothes, and anything else Mr. Grey pointed out to her.

Judy had been flying since she was fourteen. Her father a pilot himself and Judy shared his love for flying. Her Father's plane was small and much older than the company owned ones so she had a lot to learn. She not only flew the planes to become familiar with them, but she tried to learn as much about them as she could, in case of a break down. Everyone was helpful and willing to answer all her questions.

When she finally received her final approval from her flight instructor, she was elated. There was so much to do and such a short time to do it in. Her furniture had to be stored along with her excess clothing and anything else she wanted to keep for further use.

She shopped for appropriate clothing, shoes, and other requirements from the list that Mr. Gray helped her compile. He even suggested she take her own liquor if she liked anything special. It may not be easy to get and could be expensive.

A list of items from the workers already in Brazil was in the office and Judy helped buy the things to be taken down on the plane with her.

Anytime a plane made the trip, it was loaded with items from home. It was a way the company showed their concern for the people who worked for them and gave a close family type relationship. It went well except for the sewing and yarn items. Judy had to enlist help from some of the women in the office. She may be able to design bridges and build a skyscraper, but sewing on a button or knitting a sweater was not her thing.

As the time for leaving came close, Judy became more anxious to be on her way. She was still going to the airfield occasionally to get more flight time. Ben and Mike were the only licensed pilots, so it would be a big help having Judy ready to shoulder some of the flying responsibilities right away. The project being so far inland most of the travel was by small plane or helicopter.

Judy spent a week with her parents. They were not happy with her going to South America for a year, especially when they found it was deep in the jungles of Brazil. However, they had decided a long time ago, when she made up her mind to do something, all they could do was give her their blessings and pray for her. She was a determine young lady and all the talking in the world would not change her mind. She assured them she would be home for a visit at Christmas and if she needed to she could request to return home at any time.

Judy had some ideas spinning around in her head already for design but could not start anything until she studied the surroundings. The thing that gave her the most worry though, was her wardrobe. She knew it was hot and humid. She would not be able to dress in her usual feminine cool clothing, so she chose with care, trying to keep a low profile on her well-rounded figure. It would be so easy if she were a tall thin person. When they put on pants and shirt they looked like a young man, not so for Judy, she was gifted with a full bosom, small waist and rounded hips. Well, she would just have to work with what she had and choose clothes that did not call attention to that fact.

Chapter 5

The day for the departure finally came. The plane was loaded after checking and rechecking the manifest. There would be someone to meet her at the airport when she arrived in Manaus, Brazil to make arrangements for the larger items to be taken inland by truck. They were scheduled for an afternoon takeoff so they would arrive in Brazil early the next morning. That would leave plenty of time to load the supplies and return to the job site the same day. She was mentally going over all the little gifts, the messages and items she was carrying to the people, especially that dam pipe tobacco. She had forgot it and at the last minute had to sandwich it among her personal belongings. She would smell like tobacco for days. By morning she would be in Brazil, and by afternoon she would be in a remote area of jungle which was to be home for the next year. Two months ago she would never believed it possible.

The plane was equipped with reclining seats for sleeping, but she was to excite to settle down and wished for company so he decided to fix some snacks and join the crew for a while. There was so many supplies and equipment on board;

she had a difficult time reaching the little kitchen. Finally getting to where she could work, it didn't take long for the sweet aroma of fresh brewed coffee to fill the cabin.

When she took the coffee and snacks forward the captain said, "I wondered if you were going to share that coffee I could smell."

CHAPTER 6

She stayed up front with the crew and talked until long after dark and the exhaustion from the day finally caught up with her. She excused herself and settled down for some rest. The next thing she knew one of the men was shaking her awake. They would be landing within the hour and he thought she might want to freshen up.

As they landed and taxied to a position across the strip from the commercial aircraft they came to a halt in front of a small building. As the door opened and Judy followed the men off the plane, devastating humidity and heat overwhelmed her. She had never been where air was so heavy and hot, it was breathtaking. After a few minutes she was not so overpowered by it, but she was glad she had taken Mr. Grays advice and wore a sleeveless top and loose fitting cotton pants. Almost immediately they were clinging to her skin, wet from perspiration.

She checked off all the supplies and luggage as it was unloaded. The pilot had been in contact with Mike before landing and he was expected any minute. The Crew waited with her to see if Mike or Ben had anything to send back to the head office. They would spend the night in Manaus and return home tomorrow.

Judy stood close by the supplies as she watched a tall light haired man come in their direction. Judging him to be around thirty-five years old, he had a casual carefree walk and a big smile. As he approached, he said, "Hi Richard, How is it back in God's country?"

Richard reached for the outstretched hand as he greeted the tall good looking man and turned as he said, "Meet Judy, your new Architect."

She smiled and shook his hand as he said, "Wow, Ben and I expected a woman, but we didn't expect both brains and beauty."

Judy laughed at his reaction and mumbled a polite 'Thank you Mr. Downs".

"Hey, call me Mike, we'll be working and living close, so might as well do away with the formalities. Let's see what we can get on the Old Iron-hoarse, and get the remainder on its way overland."

"Richard, here's a bag of mail and some reports for you to take back," Mike said as a dark short man approached with a big canvas bag.

Richard took the bag as he said good-by to Judy. He turned and as Judy watched him walk away she thought to herself, "There goes my last tie with the good old USA for a while."

Picking up the tube container holding her drawings, she turned to Mike and handed him the manifest and said

"Let's get this show on the road," as she pitched her drawings on the plane.

She had sorted the things as they came of the plane, but wanted Mike to double check her to make sure she didn't miss any items he wanted on the plane.

Mike looked it over and agreed with her decision.

The man that came with Mike was introduced as Juan, one of our workers. "Juan, you start with the large pile. You and Jack get it on the truck and head out as soon as you can. Judy and I will load the plan, eat and be on our way. We'll see you back at camp in a few days."

Juan smiled and nodded his head at Judy as he walked away.

Mike turned to Judy, "Ben and Carl are away and won't be back until late tonight. I don't want to be away too long, so if you are ready we will get busy."

Judy was use to doing heavy work, so she had no problem lifting most of the boxes. The larger ones they lifted together and after half of it was loaded, they were both dripping wet and her hair was sticking to her forehead.

Mike said, " Slow down, you're not use to this heat. Get in the plane and see if you can arrange for more room. I'll put the rest on."

Judy did as Mike suggested and before too long the remainder of the supplies was loaded. Mike stuck his head in with that same appealing smile, "I'll bet you pack a mean suitcase 'Pumpkin Head'.

Judy glared at him, but with that boyish teasing grim, she couldn't hold a straight face.

"I hail from Northern California, your hair in the sunshine reminds me of the pumpkins laying in the field just before harvesting. I just couldn't resist calling you 'Pumpkin Head'. How about me buying you a tall, cold, drink so we can start getting use to each other and show you I am only being friendly?"

"A cold drink would go a long way right now."

"We can have a bite to eat if you like or we can wait until we get back home and it cools off a little. There will be plenty of help unloading. The crew will be so happy to see it, they will practically have everything unloaded before we get off the plane."

Judy was happy she wouldn't have to unload it all. Mike was right when he said she wasn't use to the heat and humidity. She was having a hard time breathing. This altitude and humidity would take some getting use to.

Mike heading in the direction of a small restaurant across the strip at a fast pace when Judy stopped, and yelled, "Wait! I have short legs and can't keep up with you in this heat."

Mike stopped and turned to face her, with that same 'heart stopping' smile. As he reached for her hand, he said, "Just give me a tug Pumpkin, if I go too fast for you."

Judy stared into deep brown eyes for a minute, trying to decide if his remark meant anything other than walking.

They covered the remaining distance at a reasonable pace.

At the restaurant, Judy declined the offer of anything to eat, and had only a cold drink, while absorbing the quaint surroundings. It was almost ten o'clock when they headed back to the plane and in a short time they were airborne.

The trip would take around two hours she was told, and when Judy offered to do the flying, Mike was more than happy to let her. It would be a good chance to become familiar with the route she would be flying in the future.

They talked and got aquatinted as they traveled. Judy was pleased that Mike was so easy to talk to. She ask about Ben and Mike said, "He will take some getting use to. I'm afraid he is not to crazy about women, especially in the field, but me, I love them," he laughed.

The sun was high in the sky when they reached their destination. Mike said they were to land in a few minutes, but Judy could not see anything but tree tops. Surly the airstrip would be in view by now.

All of a sudden there it was, closed in all around by jungle. You were almost on top of it when it came in view. A few degrees one way or the other you could easily miss it.

Mike gave Judy a few tips on landing, then said, "Ok, Pumpkin take her in."

The little plane was a dream to fly. After circling once she landed and in a few minutes had taxied to a smooth halt

Chapter 7

As Mike had predicted there was a welcoming committee on hand to unload everything. Along with a few "wolf whistles" and some good-hearted kidding, Judy was helped from the plane. There were brief introductions before the men unloaded the plane under Mikes' supervision. The men made a quick job of getting everything on a truck that was standing by.

Some of the personal items were doled out to eager recipients; the rest of the supplied and things were to be taken to the storage area.

Mike took out two bottles of whiskey and handed it to the men. "We'll have to share until the truck arrives, so go easy on this.

Judy was aware again of the friendly ties among the men. Mike had pointed out on the flight over that if a worker came in from the 'States' and caused friction or could not get along with the other men, he was sent back home. "It is necessary to get along, we can't have trouble or dissention, it effects everyone on the project," he had said.

"Let's head for the trailers and get out of this heat. Millie will have something for us to eat and we can relax until it cools off. Millie is Carl's' wife. We better take some of her supplies, she will be expecting it. She knits, sews, cooks and mothers us all. She makes everyone a cake on his or her birthday, she is a great lady. If you need a friend or woman to talk to, Millie is always there for you."

"She sounds like a pretty special person."

"You aren't too bad yourself lady."

Judy smiled as they walked along at a slow pace toward the first of the several trailers. She had noticed as they landed, it was like a small town, with the trailers lined up on both sides of a road leading towards, what Judy presumed, was the direction of the mine. There were small and large ones, but one thing she noticed, all had screened porches.

As they approached the first trailer a middle age lady came out of the screen porch to meet them. Mike raised his hand in a friendly wave as he greeted her. "Hi Millie! I have someone I want you to meet, she comes bearing gifts from home."

"This is Judy Winston our new Architect. I told her all about you and how you boss us all around."

Millie gave Mike a slap on the back and said, "You won't get a birthday cake next month if you keep up that lying."

She turned to Judy, still smiling a big friendly smile as she said, "Pleased to meet you Judy, welcome to Brazil. I can see things are going to heat up around here. If you have any problems, you come to me. It will take the men a while to adjust to a fellow worker being so darn cute, but I put my money on you. Come on in and have a bite to eat and a cold drink before you go up to settle in."

Judy was thankful for the refreshments; her long journey was beginning to tell on her.

Feeling a little better after having a sandwich and cold ice tea, Judy ask Millie if she was the one who requested all the sewing materials and yarns. "Yes, and anything you brought will be appreciated, I intend to make curtains for everyone."

"I had to have help on selecting all the material and yarn. I can call out the exact amount of lumber for a house but don't ask me how much yarn it takes to make a sweater. I never had the patients to learn. One of the girls at the office helped ."

Millie laughed and assured her, no matter what she brought it would be put to good use. "We aren't as big on design down here as long as it is cool and easy to care for, it will be used."

"We better go on up and get Judy settled in Millie, you can talk more later."

Judy and Mike walked up to some larger trailers lined up along a dirt road. Mike and Ben have the large double trailer and Judy was to occupy the small one next to them. There was one for an office and other workers lived in the rest. There were eight mobile homes in all. Mike helped Judy put her personal belongings in the trailer she was to live in and them they took her work supplied over to the trailer used as an office and work trailer. There was a large drafting table the length of one wall.

As they were walking back, Mike said, "Why don't you go shower and rest a little, then come over for a cool drink. We usually don't eat until after dark when it cools down. Ben should be back by them and we can all get aquatinted."

"Sounds great, see you in a while."

Judy closed the door behind her, then with both hands in tight fists, looking heavenly and with an exuberant, "Yes!", as she released some of the built up excitement

Chapter 8

After she showering and changed, she went across to Mikes trailer. She had been going non-stop since she left New York. With the time change, climate and every

thing else, her head was throbbing.

Mike was mixing them a drink, Judy had dressed in a cool lime green sundress, she had her head back and eyes closed fighting a headache of all headaches, when she heard a door open. She opened her eyes and saw a man about the same age as Mike walking across the room He was over six feet tall, thick black hair and full black mustache. He had the bluest eyes she had ever seen, or was it the dark tan and his dark hair that accented the blue eyes to make them more noticeable. Judy sat staring as he came further into the room.

She raised her head off the back of the sofa and was about to stand up when she heard him swear under his breath .

Mike came in, a drink in each hand, "Ben, Your back! Just in time to have a drink with Judy and I. Judy, This is Ben. Ben meet our new Architect."

Judy stood up to reach out her hand, before she could, he turned on his heels and headed for the liquor cabinet. He growled, "What the hell is Stew thinking of?" He stopped at the cabinet to pour himself a drink. Judy stood and stared at his back as he said to Mike, "Why didn't you send her back on the same plane she came on?"

"Come on Ben, cool down."

"I am cool! I mean it! You should have fired her and sent her back as soon as you saw her. This is no place for someone like her".

"Ben, I did not hire her, so I couldn't fire her."

I didn't hire her either, but you can sure as hell bet I would have seen she was back on that plane if I had gone to Manaus to meet her.

Judy was furious and had taken just about enough. With both hands on her hips, she stood directly in front of Ben and with vengeance she informed him, "You would have had one hell of a fight if you had tried, Mr. Roads, and I dough even you would have succeeded. Mr. Hardell hired me personally, and until I hear otherwise, he will be the one who fires me. You don't make out the pay checks and although I have to work under you, my initial orders come from the head office."

"Ben, cool off, you aren't even giving her a chance."

They both turned to look at Mike as though he had just appeared out of nowhere.

The tension eased slightly.

"Mike you know working down here is hell. It is not for anyone like her."

"Maybe so my man, but like she said, Stew hired her and he expects us to at least try and work together."

Ben looked at Judy, "Did you bring the parts for the equipment?"

Judy ask in the same tone, Did you order them?" She stared him down as she waited and when he gave a slight nod, "Then they are here," she calmly stated. "All the orders were filled and I brought all the equipment and parts on the plane. I figured they were the most important. I sorted the things I felt less important to come by truck. I brought a few items of personal nature. I did manage to pack a few days supply of your favorite tobacco that Mr. Hardell sent at the last minute. It had to be packed in my suitcase along with my clothing. I brought it over few minutes ago. It's on the counter. My clothes reek of tobacco. Anything else, Mr. Roads?"

Ben had to admit to himself; she had guts, standing up to him like that. Her face was a pale washed our color from the changes her system had to go through to get here. She looked good enough to eat in that green dress and those green eyes and creamy white skin. She reminds him of a soft, beautiful little kitten. "Dam it! She was too delicate for a position such as this. She at least deserved a chance to settle in a little. He could give her a few days but he sure as hell was going to talk to "Stew" about her.

Ben stood very still, looking at Judy with those ice blue eyes and it looked as though he was going to laugh. Her head was still throbbing from long hours without sleep and the climate change It was taking its toll on her. The stillness had almost the same effect on her as a piercing noise.

Finally smiling slightly and in a calm voice, Ben broke the silence, "Call me Ben, and you are right, I was out of line. I'm sorry. It has been a bad day here as well. How about let's start over again Judy and then I won't feel so guilty when I smoke some of that tobacco. It may calm me down a bit as well."

"Fair enough. All I want is a chance to do what I was sent down here for. I don't expect extra privileges or consideration, and I'll do what you say as far as the job goes. If I feel I can't accomplish what I was hired for I will be the first to let you know. Mr. Hardell assured me you were a fair man and would give me a fair chance."

"Well, with that, I think it is as good a time as any to make my exit I need a shower bad. Have you two eaten?'

"No, Judy and I just got cleaned up. I was about to see what Marie left. Go get your shower, we'll have it ready by the time you finish."

Mike headed for the kitchen, as he passed Judy he winked and said, "You won round one Punkin."

Judy wasn't too sure of that. Ben was undecidedly against her being on the job. Everyone held him in high respect and he did appear to be trying to be fair with her. Giving her a chance to prove herself just might be his way of showing her he is right. He certainly got her adrenaline flowing.

Chapter 9

She liked Mike. He was a fun, easy going and seemed to be a good nature guy. She had no problem communicating with him but it looked like Ben on the other hand, at the very first encounter, raised conflicts and tension. Maybe it was because he startled her, or more the other way, she startled him. She should have not dressed so feminine for their first encounter. The change from startled to anger in one easy move she was going to have to keep a tighter rein on her temper and do the best job she knew how. She was so engrossed in thought, when Mike spoke to her she jumped.

"You sure you're ok?'

"Yes, I just have a frightful headache and I'm terribly hungry."

As Ben walked back into the room, they were just finishing with the preparations for dinner. They all sat down and ate in silence for a while. Mike started asking about various people at the home office and about changes that might have occurred. Mostly just small talk, so when he looked up and inquired about her headache she realized it no longer hurt.

She laughed, "I guess it was from hunger, because it is gone now. I will have to admit, it has been a long day as well as an adjustment."

Mike said, "Yes, and I pushed you too hard at the airport. The altitude and heat down here are difficult to adjust to and I forgot to take it into consideration you had not gotten use to it yet. I saw you all glassy eyed and pale at the airport, I got a little worried. You bounced back real quickly after I poured liquid into you and gave you a little rest. Your headache was my fault as well as hunger. You will have to go slow for a few days and become adjusted to the climate. We don't want you having a heat stroke on us."

"I won't. I usually know my limits, I have learned to resist too much pressure from outside, it's the pressure within that I haven't learned to control. Unfortunately, I drive myself harder than most individuals. I guess it comes from taking on a job that was believed only men could do. I feel I must do better or best at all times."

Ben was listening with interest at Judy and Mike. It sounded like she was more capable of adjusting than her appearance suggested. God, she was an attractive lady, he would have a time keeping his men under control, hell, he couldn't even keep his eyes off her.

Mike was not one to embellish on things, so she must have carried her weight and she sure put me in my place when I questioned her responsibility as far as supplies were concerned. God! She is delicate looking and down right pretty when she gets mad. This is going to be one hell of a year. Stew knew exactly what he was doing all the time. He and Mike had worked for him over ten years and he would not send anyone down that did not have top qualifications for the job, and he could get almost anyone he wanted, so why her?

Chapter 10

Ben had not entered into the conversation, he remained quiet and although Judy tried to ignore it, she knew he was listening and watching her all threw dinner. His cool blue eyes were focused on her every time she looked up, yet he never spoke. She wished she knew what he was thinking.

Judy finally had to get up and move away to collect herself. His silence was getting on her nerves.

"I brought some of the latest hit tapes, would you like to hear some music?"

Again it was Mike who answered her. Judy took her time as she went to get them. The longer she took maybe Ben would take himself off to bed or something. She sure felt uncomfortable in his presence.

Taking the tapes and her small 'Boom-Box', she walked back slowly to their trailer. As she approached, the aroma of pipe tobacco filled her nostrils. The smoke drifting through the hot humid air had an intoxicating effect. Ben was sitting with his feet up just inside the screen porch as she opened the door to go in.

He had the pipe in his mouth, but as she entered he removed it with a little salute, "Thanks again, it is one of the things that I depend on to relax me."

Judy just nodded her head to show she hear him and continued inside to play the music without comment.

They listened to music as she and Mike cleaned the table. A short time later Judy returned to her place for the night. As she passed Ben still smoking on the porch she simply wished him goodnight.

Mike had asked her if she wanted to go out in the morning to check out the sites for the plant and housing or wait a day or two. She was anxious to get started and told him as much. Plans were made to meet at about seven in the morning.

Chapter 11

Later in her own trailer, Judy lay awake a long time replaying the encounter with Ben. It seemed she had just drifted off when the alarm went off, however, she was up and dressed by six-thirty in her kaki shirt, pants and special boots. They were like a hiking boot but with steel toes. She felt like she was all feet. Her hair was loose, to cover her neck from the sun. It was just before seven when she picked up her helmet and went out the door.

Ben and Mike were coming out the door as she went across with her plans for the plant in her hand. They were dressed in tan cotton outfits, similar to hers and as she approached them she felt dwarfed. Her sandals had given her a little height, but the boots were flat. Standing next to the two men who were both over six feet, she felt uncomfortable.

Ben shook his head and before he thought about it, he said, "God, But you are little."

Just as he said it he saw her eyes light up and before she could comment, he held both hands in the air, palms facing

33

her as if he was pushing her away, "Don't get all worked up, no offence meant."

She laughed as she said, "No offence taken."

Judy followed the two men toward a Jeep Wrangler with oversized mud tires. The step up had to be at least three feet. It was worse than mounting a horse. She was attempting to get a hand hold on something to pull herself up, when her waist was seized in a vice-like grip, her feet left the ground, she flew through the air towards the back seat of the jeep. She landed in the seat so furious she could have hit Ben over the head with one of her steel-toed boots.

They sped off so fast she was pinned to the seat, which was a good thing. It gave her time to calm her anger towards Ben and his high handed help. She figured Mike, who was driving, did it for that reason.

They stopped at Carl and Millie's to pick Carl up to go with them. Judy liked Carl and his wife. They were friendly and nice. Millie was standing on the porch and waved as they drove away. Carl had jumped in the back seat with Judy.

"How do you feel today Kiddo?"

"Rested and ready to work. Is it far to the area?"

"Not far, we put our living quarters just far enough away so we wouldn't have to move when we started construction. We could walk it, but the heat and humidity gets bad by noon. We have cleared a road, if you have to walk it, be sure you stay to the middle. Snakes and insects like to sun themselves in the road. Make plenty of noise and they scurry away," he laughed. " Millie said to tell you, if you get a cut or scratch, no matter how small, you let her help you see to it. Infection can get out of hand real fast down here."

"I will, tell her thanks."

Ben said, "We will check the housing area today so Carl and his men can start clearing some it if it meets with your approval."

It was less than a mile and Judy was glad. Her bottom was going to be sore. The road was rough and bumpy and Mike didn't seem to care if he hit every rut at top speed.

Some of the men were going to the mine to work as they arrived. There were tents and some had only lean-to type covers to sleep under. Any type of housing would be an improvement and best of all; they would be able to have their families with them when housing was completed. Some of the Hardell men were there, clearing the ground of brush and vines.

Judy got out as Ben started barking orders. "Carl, you help Judy get all the measurements she needs and go over the grounds with her. I will take her tomorrow and check out the plant site. We want to get the roads in as soon as possible. If you need anything let us know. Don't work past eleven. Take her back to the trailer to work inside in the afternoons for a while. We'll be around if you need us."

"Right Ben, We'll be fine, I'll keep a keen eye on our little lady."

"Careful how you refer to her size and gender, she is a little sensitive about both Carl." Ben said as he started off in the opposite direction, laughing to himself.

"Pompous male."

Carl just smiled and didn't say anything. He introduced her to several men who were working on the backhoes and tractors, clearing and leveling the ground. They worked steadily until almost eleven. Judy felt they had accomplished a great deal. It would not take her long to give them enough to keep them busy until she was ready to put it all together. She and Carl had lined out where the roads would be and the first thing she needed to draw up was the layout for trenches so they could get the sewer pipes and utility lines in as soon as possible. The clearing was almost finished. She would go over the trash to energy plant plans and get started on it, then when it was well under way , then housing could soon follow.

Chapter 12

She decided she could easily work around most of the trees, leaving them for shade and comfort. None of the age-old trees would be sacrificed. They had done a good job searching out a site for the housing. By positioning the houses right, the trees would help keep the homes and plant cooler. Judy was beginning to see the little town take shape in her mind already and was anxious to start putting it down on paper when Carl informed her it was lunchtime. She hadn't even thought about food until he mentioned it, then her stomach rumbled in response. She was glad to see most of the house plans she had started on would work with very few changes.

Carl was a better driver than Mike, at least he drove slower and attempted to miss some of the bumps. Carl insisted she have lunch with he and Millie, so after she freshened up she walked across. Her thoughts were on the plans and she was so excited she wanted to share it with them. She talked the whole time Millie was putting lunch on the table and continued right through their eating. She had explained the "trash to energy " plant and how she wanted to save every tree she could. When Carl announced he would have to go back to work, Judy was embarrassed that she had monopolized their lunch hour.

"Carl, I'm sorry I talked so much, it's just that I am so excited."

"You just keep up the way you are, I can see why Stewart hired you. You take your time here and them go on over to the drafting tables when you feel like it. We will have that clearing ready for you when you are ready to go."

"Thanks Carl."

Judy visited a while longer with Millie, then she walked across to the work trailer. She worked on sketches to get the complete idea down on paper. She was surprised at how fast it came together. She had spent many hours thinking about it while she was preparing to come to Brazil and it paid off. She was taking advantage of the large workspace. A sketch of the township and plant was at one end of the big drafting table, spread so she could refer to the location of the trees, where she had laid the roads and the housing lots. She was using the same plans from the job in Canada for the plant so there were only a few changes to adjust to this project. By late afternoon she was ready to work on floor plans for the homes. They needed to be simple but functional, so there was very little work to drawing up various plans. They would be similar in design but vary in size.

CHAPTER 13

Because of her small size, Judy had a bad habit of putting her feet through the rungs of the stool to rest her feet. Her boots were heavy and she was sitting, toes hooked from inside around the rung of the stool. She was so engrossed in her work she did not hear anyone approaching.

When Ben spoke, he was behind her looking over her shoulder. He gave her such a start she jumped and tried to stand. With the heavy boots on, struggling to free her feet, the stool started to tip over with her on it. Ben caught her before she landed face first on the floor. The stool hit the floor with a bang. Ben stood with her in his arms. Judy's heart was beating as fast as a hummingbirds and her face grew hot. She knew it must be flushed. As Ben held her, he was aware of her as a very desirable woman. What was he thinking? As he slowly put her down and released the hold on her, he chastised himself. Smiling, he reached for the stool. Judy still disoriented reached for it at the same time. They were close. She could smell the masculine odor that surrounded him. He gently laid a hand on her arm, "Let me."

Smiling and with a teasing voice he said "You really should be more careful, I may not always be here to catch you".

"I am usually not so clumsy, you startled me. I was concentrating so much I didn't hear you come in."

"You must be exhausted, we came back hours ago. I saw the lights on in the work area and came to investigate.

Judy looked at her watch and was surprised at the time. She had worked right through dinnertime and it was getting dark outside.

"Call it a day and come meet everyone."

"We're firing up the grill and getting steaks ready to cook. Leave it for now, it will give you a chance to meet all the workers."

They went out the door. Mike was sitting in the driver seat with the jeep engine running. As they approached the jeep, Judy again was grabbed and hoisted up and over the front seat. Ben jumped in without saying a word and they took off.

Before going anywhere with Ben again, she decided, there was going to be an understanding about letting her get in any mode of transportation on her own steam. Now was not the time. She could see everyone gathered in Millie and Carl's yard.

"We have cold drinks and beer on ice or there is ice tea for the non drinkers," Mike offered as they walked up and greeted some of the workers.

Judy took a cold beer and went in search of Millie to see if she needed any help, she also wanted to get some output on what was needed in the homes. Millie, having been in Brazil longest, would have a good idea of the necessities.

Millie was relaxing in a rocking chair with some of her knitting close by. Judy laughed and said; "I visualized you over a hot stove, running yourself ragged cooking for this crowd.

"Lands no, we put potatoes on the grill and open some beans. When the men feel the need they put the meat on the grill. We just help our self until we are full or it is all gone. The men are use to taking care of themselves down here."

Judy and Millie talked about what was needed in the homes and how much area for each individual house. She was a great help and although there was very little difference in what she had already decided and what Millie suggested, it was good to have another opinion. Sometimes what looks good on paper is not all that practical in real life.

"Looks like the men are hungry. The meat is going on the grill. Let's go down and give them a hand."

Judy joined Mike and started helping him, laughing and joking with the men and enjoying her self. Mike was tending the meat so Judy went to get him another cold beer. Just as she reached the tub of iced drinks, Ben appeared next to her. He had been watching her laughing and talking to all the men and for some reason it had him ready to reprimand her. "Don't get too familiar with the men, it could lead to trouble. There are too many men who will read your friendliness wrong, so go easy."

"I know how to handle myself, so don't worry about me."

"I am not worrying about you. I just don't want to lose a good man because of personal problems. It is too hard to get workers and I know men. So just cool the joking and laughing so much."

He turned and walked away before Judy could defend herself anymore. It made her furious, but in essence she knew he was right. She had already thought that very thing. That is exactly why she had walked away .

She used getting a beer for Mike as an excuse to back off without it being obvious. If Mr. High and Mighty had stayed around she would have told him so too. Now he would think it was his idea. Well, let him. She didn't need his personal acceptance to do a good job. One thing for certain he was going to hear of her disapproval of him throwing her in that stupid jeep ever time she went with him. Judy took Mike's beer to him just as he announced the food was ready. Everyone was so busy eating, and no one noticed when she wandered off to join Millie.

To insure no other encounter with the boss, Judy ate with Carl and Millie. Ben ate with some of the men.

Mike came over and sat down, "You and Ben seem to bring out the worst in each other. What was that all about at the ice tub?"

"Nothing, we just don't seem to be able to agree on much of anything. Don't worry Mike it will work out. I'm still getting settled in. When the building gets underway everything will be ok."

"I hope so Punkin, I like you and don't want to see you leave."

"Don't worry, there is not a chance of that. I came to do a job and I intend to see it through to the end."

As the sun went down the mosquitoes and bugs came out in force. It was not long after eating that everyone drifted off to his or her sleeping quarters.

She was anxious to put some of her ideas on paper and the quiet, cool, little trailer was just the place to do it.

Chapter 14

She had drawn up the plans for the plant back home while she was preparing for her trip.

Tomorrow she was to go with Ben to examine the area they had chosen for the plant and see if she approved and see if there were any changes necessary before they could get started on it. The plant would have to be completed and up and running before the homes could be occupied. She left designing the houses until she arrived in South America. She wanted to look over the land before she stated the homes. Judy figured three or four floor plans where all she would needed.

Once they started the plant she would not be needed as much there and would have more time to work on the homes. She wanted to be ready with the housing plans so Carl's men would not have to wait for them when some came available as the plant was near completion. If she planned it right they would clear and build the plant, them go right into the housing with no delays while Ben and Mike would oversee getting the plant up and running.

Judy worked until she could no longer hold her eyes open. She was ready to draw the plans for at least three houses and had all the 'specks' figured before she finally gave up for the night. She was exhausted and fell asleep almost the minute her head hit the pillow.

Chapter 15

Judy had loaded her plans in the jeep and was getting in when Ben came out of his trailer. He just nodded as he got in and started the engine. They drove about a mile and turned into a smaller road. The road was winding and twisting under heavy jungle like forest. At times the vines and trees were so dense, there was merely a tunnel large enough for the jeep to pass. It was beautiful. The flowers and greenery untouched by man. It was very quiet, with only the noise of the jeep breaking the silence.

"We are only about two miles from the housing. Mike and I have surveyed the area between the two points. We will have no problem running a pipeline and underground wiring between the two points. We can start with the clearing and roads as soon as the final site is set."

He had stopped. "From this point on to the river, you can start searching out a site for your plant. I will drive the section as many times as you feel necessary. We will make a complete run down and back first, the second time if you want to stop just let me know. Sound ok to you?"

"That's fine. I can't believe the beauty of all this. How did you find this place? Was there a trail already here or did you make it?"

"No trail. We went up several days in the helicopter and looked things over before we settled on this area. We can go up in the helicopter and look things over before you decide if you want."

"You two are the engineers, I only design and build. You know what is necessary from the briefs I sent down. I trust your expertise enough to accept your decision."

Judy was looking from one side to the other, concentrating on the land as they were going down the road for the third time and did not see Ben's expression when she made the 'matter of fact' statement. She had pulled a pad out of her backpack and had a pencil poised, ready to take notes.

The fourth time, as they moved slowly away from the river, she ask him to stop for a few minutes then as they continued on she made a few notes. She finally selected a large clearing about half way up from the river. Judy asks if they could get out of the jeep.

As they did he cautioned her of the dangers, he and Mike had only cleared a road to inspect the possibilities.

"I like this clearing. It appears to be large enough and is ideally located."

Judy did not miss Ben's look of admiration this time.

"Mike and I liked it also, we did a few test samples of the soil, it is solid and without rocks. The sun angle is what you ask for and water is nearby. Flowing water, preferably, Right?" Ben had quoted her specifications exactly. She had sent them down weeks ago from the head office while she was still being prepared for her trip.

"I appreciate you letting me select the site without trying to influence my decision. It seems three minds are in agreement. Unbelievable!" she laughed as she propelled her feet up and over the side of the jeep landing on the ground in one graceful move, taking her back pack with her. She laid it on the hood of the jeep and removed her camera. Ben got out and started taking some things out of the back of the jeep.

"If we go off the road, I go first. I want to make sure there are no dangers lurking in the brush. What do you have in mind?"

"I need some pictures of the area mostly. I am sure there is ample space but we can walk off or guess pretty close to the size of the clearing and make sure there is enough land to place the plant on this site properly."

"There is over the amount you specified and it is almost square. You can place it any direction. There is one very large old tree at the far corner that could be a problem. We can go down, check it out, then work our way back if you want."

"Sounds like a good plan to me that way I can get everything I need."

While Judy was organizing what she needed, Ben opened some can meat to have with some crackers before they went to work.

They headed across the field towards a large tree in the far corner. It was a huge magnificent old tree, centuries old. There was no way she would destroy something as great as that old tree to build a waste to energy plant. If she couldn't work the plant on the property with the tree still standing, she would just have to find another plot of land.

Judy stopped occasionally to take pictures and jot down information, always aware of where she stepped. It was important to note where each picture was taken and how far from the last one. From what she had seen so far, she was sure this location was ideal and Ben was right, there was more than enough space to avoid the old tree.

Mr. Hardell was right, Ben and Mike were good at their job. If they needed more land they could move the road over some and take out some smaller less important growth on that side.

Ben was chopping and beating down the brush, making enough noise to raise the dead as well as sleeping serpents.

As they approached the tree, there was less brush and more low green moss like ground cover. Large roots from the age-old tree penetrated the earth, rising high enough to make comfortable benches. They were soaked from perspiration and welcomed the cool shade of the old tree. Sitting on one of the roots, Judy removed her sun helmet and raised her hair off her neck. Ben watched as she used the helmet to fan her flushed face. She took her small canteen of water out of her pack. After taking a few sips, she offered it to Ben.

Ben took it as he wondered if she knew how desirable she looked, sitting there under that old tree with her hair raised up by an arm that caused her shirt to pull tight across her full breasts.

"Thanks I left mine in the jeep. Not too smart for someone in charge."

"No big deal, it will come in handy when we work our way back to the jeep."

"Better take your pictures, a storm is starting to materialize. That is why it's hot and humid. You have heard of the, 'Quiet before the storm'. I think it originated in Brazil."

Judy started to work, while Ben settled himself against the tree with his pipe. Judy suspected he was dozing, as there was no movement from him for some time.

She decided she had enough, when she spotted a huge branch, not too far off the ground. If she could get up on it she could take an aerial type picture, which would be very helpful.

Strapping her camera over her back to make the climbing easier, she started climbing. It was higher than it looked. It was a struggle but she finally reached the limb where she could get a good hold. It was easy swinging her legs up over the big limb. She stood up and took several pictures. The wind was starting to blow, thunder and lightning was all around them now. She was getting ready to get down when Ben appeared below her.

"What is hell are you doing up there?" He was mumbling other things, which at this point, Judy was sure it was better she could not hear him.

"No problem, I can swing down. Here take my camera so I don't drop it."

Ben took the camera and laid it out of the way. "Swing down, I'll help you."

Judy would rather do it alone, but in his mood she decided it best to not argue. She laid over on her stomach and started easing herself closer to the ground. She had just slid all the way off the limb with her body and was getting a handhold to swing down when she felt that familiar vice like grip around her legs. It startled her so she released her hand too soon from the limb. Ben must have been off balance or he underestimated her weight, either way, he fell backwards, taking her with him. Judy landed with a 'thud' smack on top of his chest.

"Damn Him! Judy was furious, "I probably killed the big lug."

She had heard his breath escape in a big gush, like the very life had been pushed out of him.

She moaned, "With my weight I probably crushed his ribs, or whatever one does by landing on top of someone."

She rolled off him and kneeled beside him. There was no movement or sign of life.

"Damn!" "Ben!…. Ben!… she shook him, patted his cheeks, "Ben, damn you don't you be hurt."

Still no answer or movement from the prone figure on the ground.

"Great! What do I do now?" He was twice her size and the jeep was five hundred yards away. She was contemplating going for the jeep, but even if she brought it closer, there was no way she could lift him. She had to do something, that storm was moving in fast. She was patting some of the water from her canteen on his face when she saw the corner of his mouth move slightly.

"You beast," he was conscious and working hard at suppress his laughter. With her hand clenched in a fist she hit him hard on the muscular upper arm. She immediately regretted it, his arm was as solid as a rock, and pain shot up her arm from the blow she threw. Ben's face was filled with amusement watching her shake her hand in pain. He stared to laugh. She was so relieved he was ok she started laughing herself.

They were both laughing uncontrollably, Judy fell forward placing her open palms on his chest for support. Ben was still flat on his back, as she leaned over him. Their eyes met. He reached for her as their laughter faded. The storm clouds covered them like a blanket as the thunder rumbled around them.

"You are one lethal lady."

Ben pulled her to him, Judy's mind pulled away but her body surrendered to his touch. It was as though she had no control of her own body. Judy knew he was going to kiss her, as their lips met, Ben rolled, taking her with him. Judy locked her arms around his neck holding on as though her life depended on not letting go. She felt like she was still falling from the tree and had not hit bottom.

Judy was on her back in the grass, Ben's lips softly teased hers when he stopped and looked in her eyes. "Damn"

Judy could not be sure if the white flashes of light was lightening or her own response to his kisses. Judy's senses returning to normal about the same time as Ben's must have, she began to realize the damage of their passionate encounter. Being shielded by Ben's body, she didn't realize until he moved away slightly, he had been protecting her from the downpour of rain. The storm had arrived at a good time it seemed.

Ben laughed as he jumped up, pulling her with him. They quickly gathered their belongings and ran for the road. By the time they were safely in the jeep, they were drenched and their clothes were heavy from the soaking rain. The exertion and the steamy atmosphere left them exhausted and out of breathe.

They sat for a few minutes, resting. Judy had never seen such a raging storm. It was freighting. It rained so hard she couldn't even see the trees a short distance away.

As Ben started the jeep, he said, "I can't believe I was stupid enough to be caught out in this. As long as I have worked in South America, I know the dangers and should have avoided it. We will be lucky if we don't get stuck someplace before we get out of here."

Judy looked at Ben, his hands clutching the steering wheel so tight his knuckles were white. He turned to look at her as they moved slowly down the trail. "Don't worry I will get you back safe."

Ben was concentrating on his driving but it did not prevent him from chastising himself for kissing Judy. That was a stupid thing to do. He warned the men to respect her and not make any trouble and he couldn't control his own stupid impulses.

Ben turned away so Judy could not see his eyes, "Judy, I am sorry, that should never have happened. I warned all the men, if they laid a hand on you, they would answer to me. I thought Mike might make a pass or one of the men, I never thought I would be the one to lose control."

He reached over the seat to retrieve a towel.

He tossed it to her and said, "Here, dry off.

He stared straight ahead, refusing to look at her, concentrating on his getting them to the main road before they got stuck. Judy didn't know what to say or think. Was it only a weak moment by a man in the jungle to long or was there really something between them. Judy was sure there was more to it, but if that was the way he wanted to play it, fine, she could to. She sure was not going to make a fool of herself over him.

"Forget it!" It could happen to anyone. It isn't as if I haven't been kissed before. A goodnight kiss from a casual date certainly did not warrant a commitment, so why should our little encounter be any different. It was a fun afternoon, nothing more, and no one need to know what went on."

She surprised herself with the unaffectedness and calmness of her voice. Ben was also. He turned to look at her but Judy was busily drying her hair and had her face covered with the towel he had tossed her.

Chapter 16

It was approaching evening when they arrived back at camp. The storm stayed with them and rain was still coming down so hard she could hardly make out the trailers. Ben parked close and they ran for the porch. They went charging into the living room, soaking wet.

Mike was not alone. "Judy! Ben! Boy are you two soaked. Hate to tell you but we have company. Antonio Ruez, our representative for the government, decided to fly over to see firsthand what was going on and to help get things underway."

Ben and Judy stood dripping all over the floor as a very elegant gentleman casually rose to meet them.

"Call me Tony, please. He shook Ben's hand, then turned to Judy and in a most gracious bow, he took her hand, "Ah, Miss Winston, I presume, the beautiful lady designer. A pleasure Senioritia, I hope we will work well together."

Judy insisted he call her Judy as she thanked him. After a few minutes of polite talk, the storm seemed to let up so she excused herself to go shower and get into some dry clothes.

She needed a few minutes to collect her thoughts. She had been so preoccupied with thoughts about Ben she was not ready to discuss other matters.

As she showered she could not help thinking about Tony Ruez. An extremely handsome man with dark olive skin and jet black hair suggested a true South American ancestry. His polite intelligent manner hinted aristocratic upbringing. Just what she need was another male to contend with as well as a boss that sent her hormones jumping.

Judy charged in on the porch with a very large umbrella protecting her from the rain. She had put on a cool sun-dress and a pair of sandals, her hair was still wet, so she pulled it back severely from her face into a bun on top of her head. Large gold earrings dangled from her ears. She was trying to achieve a look of confidence, which she certainly didn't feel.

As Judy joined the men they were discussing the project. Ben had changed as well and was sitting with a drink in hand. Mike fixed Judy one and as he handed it to her he said, "After that wetting down you need something."

Tony was interested in the project and started directing his questions to Judy. "Ben, why don't you and I put dinner on the table while Judy shows Tony some of the plans she brought over?"

"Don't take too long. It will be ready shortly."

Judy had gone over the plans thoroughly and Tony was pleased with them. They were discussing getting the material brought in.

"We will need a detail list as soon as possible," Tony was saying, just as Mike announced dinner was ready.

Judy tried not to seem too surprised at the very nice dinner laid out on the table, but as she glanced in Mike's direction, he gave a little wink and smiled as he said, "Dinner is served." Judy suspected Millie had a hand in it.

The storm was still raging outside. Judy was glad Tony had chosen this particular time to inspect things. She needed the distractions to keep her mind off the storm and off Ben.

She was so deep in thought and didn't realize Mike was talking to her.

"I'm sorry Mike, what did you say? I was listening to the storm."

"I was asking if you liked the location we found for your plant?"

"Oh Yes! It is exactly what I requested Mike. I took pictures and will start working with the drawings tomorrow. I should have the layout complete before the end of the week. Carl can start getting his equipment ready to go and I would suggest going ahead with a road from the housing area to the plant site first thing. That way we can use it rather than the roundabout way Ben and I took today.

" Will this rain last long? Do you get storms like this often?"

"No Senorita, they are not usually this violent. Are you uneasy?"

"I am not use to it is all. I'll be ok."

"The storm should pass within the hour Judy." Mike's comforting words were reassuring.

After dinner Judy helped Mike clear away the dishes and left Ben to entertain Tony. When they finished they decided to joined the other two on the porch with fresh coffee.

"It is gloriously cool."

They all laughed. "Enjoy it, tomorrow the humidity will be higher than ever after the storm Punkin."

When they came out Ben had moved to make room for Judy to sit next to him on a porch swing. She was too close to him for comfort. "I really must go over my notes and start processing the film I took, so if you gentlemen will excuse me, I'll say good night."

Tony rose, "Good Night Judy, I will be leave sometime tomorrow if I don't see you I will be in touch. Unfortunately I have other commitments. I will await your list of material and expedite it promptly. Until we meet again."

Ben watched her rise to leave and his soft voice was like a caress in the darkness, "Good Night Judy."

She walked away; not wanting to look back for fear of showing the effect his voice had on her. Why did it effect her that way and why did she care so much what Ben thought of her work? She had always been so sure of herself and felt confident in her answers. Why now, of all times, when she was being tested on a job she had dreamed of for years. As she lay in bed much later, she was still going over her problem, she knew she could do the job as well as any man. She had been in charge of harder projects back in the States.

She was almost asleep when a sudden light went on in her head. She sat upright in bed, wide-awake. "I don't give a dam about him approving of my work. I want his approval of me as a woman. I have fallen for the big lug. I can't believe I have been so dumb," As she lay back down, she thought, "Dumb indeed. One can control the mind most of the time, but how do you control the heart? He is not what I would choose using common sense. He is arrogant, chauvinistic and downright bossy. No chance of a lasting relationship with someone who jumps from one remote place to another, miles from civilization and no place to call home. I cannot get involved! I will forget all about him once I am back home and this is over." Judy drifted off into a restless sleep, with the storm gone outside, she now had one brewing within.

CHAPTER 17

The men were gone the next morning when Judy went across to work. There were keys and a note telling her they would see her later in the day. She had a vehicle at her disposal, but she was to stay close and if she left the immediate area she was to let someone know before leaving.

Where was there to go other than the swimming hole or the plant sight. Did he think she would head out in the jungle on a sightseeing tour or try to drive to town?

She had worked for a while when Carl came in. "It is so hot and humid out their today but after a few hours of work, we decided to wait until it cools off to do anymore today."

"Where are Ben and Mike?"

"They took Tony to see where the plant will be and talking over what will be needed for the pipeline from between the plant, mine and homes. He wanted to visit the mine while he was here as well, since it is one of his responsibilities as well. They should be back before noon.

"Do you think he is in favor of the project or are we going to get resistance from him?"

Having to present the project on such short notice, Judy was concerned she may not have presented information to convince him how important the plant was.

Carl studied her a minute before answering, "The way I see it, he is completely sold on the project and the designer. We are getting first priority; he is having the lumber brought in by cargo plane. He wants no delays he said."

Judy smiled, "You are kidding, right."

Carl shook his head slowly; "He was walking the area when we went up to work this morning. He said he took the liberty of looking at your drawings last night before he turned in. Millie had fixed him up in the work trailer with a bcd and the plans were still laid out from yesterday on the table. He had a lot of questions, but seemed impressed with everything so far. He does have some concern about a group that is against any progress in the area. They are probably into drugs and afraid we will disrupt there business. From what he says it is a real dangerous group and has requested extra military in to help protect us. He is particularly concerned for the women. These are ruthless men Judy and if they capture a women she is rarely found alive."

"Well as long as he is sold on the project, I will do whatever it takes to get the work going even dogged by a guard if that is necessary.

As she turned back to her work, "I don't want your men to catch up with me. "I'll work through lunch to make up for the late start."

Carl laughed as he turned to go out the door, "When you do take a break, I am sure Millie would welcome a visit."

CHAPTER 18

Judy had been working a few hours when the door opened, causing her to jump.

Ben and Tony came in. Ben went over to the desk and Tony came over where she was working.

"What are you working on?"

" This is the layout for the plant. I took pictures of the site yesterday while Ben and I looked it over and this morning I placed it on the site where I feel will be the most advantageous." These are drawings for the homes. I have been relying on input from Millie on what is needed. As soon as I complete the list of supplies for the plant, roads and pipelines for Carl, I will complete the plans and the list of material for the homes , after that I will start the drawings and plans for the guesthouse. "The guest house will be started as men get freed up from the plant and homes. It won't be too long before you will have a comfortable place to stay when you come to visit. This is a list of a few things I must add to my list of materials. I make a list as I go so I don't forget anything. Would you like to see what I have finished?"

"Very much so. I took the liberty of going over the ones on the table last night. I was impressed. I went over some things with Ben and Carl earlier. I hope you are not offended that I did not wait for you."

"Of course not. Carl told me. I realize the importance of getting this finished in record time and we all are working together to get the job done."

She spread the plans out on the table, "Did everything meet with your approval? I can make changes if you are concerned about anything, now is the time to make the change."

"Indeed, I was most pleased. The forest is to stay as it is and each home will be located in areas most suited to its size and shape. You have done an excellent job so far. The plant sight is appropriate as well. Ben and I are working out details on what you will need for the pipeline and also I will have telephone lines to you in a short time. Everything appears to be in order and ready to go."

He watched as she rolled the plans up and stored them away.

"You are a remarkable woman to come all the way down here and work in such conditions for a project such as this."

"Thank you, it is what I like to do."

She glanced in Ben's direction. He was sitting at the desk, pen in hand, looking at her. She quickly looked away as she heard the chair scrape the floor as he stood up.

"We need to talk Judy, Tony has some concerns and wants to discuss with us the problems they expect.

Tony advised them of a guerrilla group of ruthless fighters that opposed the advancement in this area. They depended on the dope trade to fund their fighting so obvious they did not want a lot of military or government representatives in the area. He stressed the importance of keeping the women and children close to camp and always be aware of the surroundings for unusual action. They were warned to notify him immediately if they had any strangers trying to enter for work or any other reason. The workers were all to be brought in after they and been approved by his department.

"It's getting late. I must go."

Judy was surprised "You're leaving?"

"Yes, I must, but I cannot stress enough the dangers here. I have other projects but I am anxious to get the 'wheels turning' here, as you would say, so your materials will be coming to you very soon. I will be returning regularly for inspections and updates and I am always only a call away. I will look forward to seeing you soon. Also I wish to invite you to visit my family in Manaus. You must take some time off?"

Judy was speechless at first, she did not want to encourage him, she was not interested in him personally but she did not want to offend him either.

"We will have to see. Right now I am too busy to even think of taking time off. Maybe a day when things get moving, my free time is very limited."

"Ben you do not insist on working seven days a week surly?"

"No Tony, my workers have Sunday off. You know that. Work permitting, two days. However, Judy is pretty much her own boss. I can't speak for her."

"You must insist she relax and not work too hard. All of you are invited to come for a visit. My parents would like to have you and we could become better acquainted."

"As Judy said, We will see how thing progress."

Ben opened the door, suggesting the subject closed.

Chapter 19

The next morning she was refreshed and ready to do battle with the drafting table.

Tony had left the night before and Ben, Mike and Carl were unloading the things she had brought down as well as some of the supplies brought from the other job they were finishing up. The men were gone when Judy came out for breakfast. That suited Judy fine. With no interruptions, work would go a lot faster.

She worked steadily for the next two days. On the third day, she was just finishing the floor plans for the first house when Mike, Ben and Carl pulled up in the jeep. It was a good time to break for lunch. She would have something to eat, then take the drawings across to show Millie and relax for a while before coming back to work.

Mike was first in the door. When he saw her at the drawing board he said, "Hey Judy! Time for lunch. Have a bite with us and let us see what you have finished."

"Mike, maybe Architects are like artist. Do architects share their work or do we have to wait for the finished product?"

Judy wasn't sure the question was for her, but Mike turned with a questioning look on his face and left her to answer.

"I just completed the final layout for the homes, plant and road system as well as the guest house. I was going to fix myself some lunch, then take the plans across for Millie to look at. I have been asking her for input and suggestions for the houses. I hope you don't mind. I feel she has a good idea of what is needed and will work best."

The plans were still spread open on the board, so Judy stepped back to let them look with a full view of the drawings. Mike flipped through the plans as Ben and Carl looked over his shoulder.

Carl walked over to the layout plans for roads and pipelines as Mike and Ben looked over the plans for the plant.

"Carl, you can take those with you if you want. I will go with you in the morning. We can go over everything to see if you think we need to change anything. You know the country better than I do, so don't hesitate to let me know if something needs changing. I am not over sensitive and am open to any suggestions that might improve the project."

"You have been a busy lady. These are great. You really know your stuff. Don't you agree Ben?"

"As you can see, I tried to save every tree and some of the natural growth. If you feel it is too hard or time consuming to grate around them, I can re-design that in no time."

Ben came over to join them at the table where they were discussing the layout. Judy again felt the need for Ben's approval. She didn't realize until he spoke, she had been holding her breath waiting for his answer.

"I agree wholeheartedly Carl, they are very good, but it is to be expected, with Stewart hiring her personally, she had to be something special. He was against women in foreign assignments almost as much as I am. Are you ready to put the men to work on the building?"

The Pompous Ass, he couldn't give a compliment without his little jab at her. Judy ignored the remark as she stuffed the plans in a carry case to take with her. She couldn't get out of his sight fast enough. How could she have thought he had any feeling for anyone especially her.

Judy started rolling up the plans, "As soon as you approve everything, they can start. Carl and I can start marking off the plant and roads and next week we should be ready to mark the foundations for the homes. That way if he wants to work both projects he can. Once we get the structure of the plant built it is mostly up to you and Mike to get the machinery installed and working. I just design them and leave what goes in them to someone else."

Carl said "I've checked and I don't see any problem with the layout just as it is. If we can save all or most of those great old trees, we will. I think my men can have the road through and the land ready by the end of the week. As soon as the plant site is grated, I will come get you to help me with the layout. I think we are ready to roll!"

"Great Carl, we'll be ready. Mike, I'll see you later, I am going over to talk to Millie about the homes."

As she started out the door, Mike said , "The rest of the crew will be along shortly and we are all going for a swim. You are welcome to join us. Be ready around three if you want to go."

"Thanks, sounds great, I'll be ready."

Judy had just finished lunch when she asks, "Millie I seem to constantly upset Ben. I can't do anything right and the more I try the more he seems dissatisfied."

"Honey you scares Ben. He has never had to deal with anyone like you and you make him uncomfortable, plus the fact that you could be a target by the rough group working in the area. You are a good looking woman and have hair and skin that they would kill for down here. He spelled it out in no uncertain terms to all the men. They are to keep their distance and respect your authority but at the same time watch out for your safety. Carl said Ben told them if there was any problems they had to answer to him. He is a good man Judy, just give it time things will get better. Now you just show me my new house and quit worrying."

Judy was ready at three when Mike came to take her swimming. She had slipped a pair of jeans and loose top over her swimsuit. Millie had said the swimming hole was some distance from the campsite. Much to her dismay, Ben was sitting in the driver seat, pipe in his mouth, his foot propped up on the door facing, waiting patiently when she went outside. A jeep with an armed guard in it was waiting to follow.

At least she would get a chance to show "Mr. High and Mighty" she could get in the jeep by herself. Mike sensed her determination and offered no assistance. She skillfully achieved her challenge and nothing was said. Ben and Mike were in swim trunks and shirts, which both had not bothered to button.

"I hope you have a swimsuit under all those clothes. There isn't much of a place to change clothes. Mike and I just wear our trunks."

"I thought it would be better if I didn't parade around in a swimsuit, I try to conceal my femininity as much as possible."

"Judy, there is no clothes made that can conceal your feminist attributes. I am not trying to be smart, just honest. You have a figure any man dreams of, your skin is like rose petals and your hair is,...." Seeing Mike smile, he realizing he had said too much already, "lets just say I don't compare it to a pumpkin as Mike does."

Mike laughed as Judy's flushed face showed her shock at Ben's remark. She couldn't say a word. They traveled in silence for a while. The beautiful green surroundings and colorful flowers were breathtaking. Judy commented on it several times.

Ben spoke, "Brazil is in a dilemma over saving their rain forest or providing for its people. Amazon is rich with minerals; the land is abundant for farm settlers and cattle. With their population growing so rapidly they are moving out of the cities and into areas like this, threatening the survival of the rain forest.

That is why we are here, there are strict laws on clearing of trees and destroying any growth without government approval. That is why we will be seeing a great deal of Tony the next few months and possibly some trouble from opposition to growth. He will keep a close eye on us to make sure we meet our commitment to his government. It could lead to other projects if they are pleased with the results on this one."

"We're here."

To her surprise, many of the workers were already there. As the jeep came to an abrupt stop, Mike jumped out and reached for Judy's hand, not realizing as she stepped down she was being watched by everyone to see her reaction. There was a pool about fifty yards across, the water was so still it was like a mirror reflecting the tall green forest around it. On the far side there was a fall of crystal clear water pouring over the side of a large rock, hardly making a sound as it quietly replenished the pool with fresh clear water.

"It's breathtaking."

Mike was the first to break the silence; "We all felt the same when we first discovered it. We had it tested before anyone was allowed in. It is as pure as it looks. We do share it with a few fish that like to nibble so don't be afraid, they are not of the perinea species. Come on lets go in and cool off. You can swim can't you?"

"Can a bird fly? I grew up on the beach. I swim better than I walk Mike."

They stripped to their swimsuits and as they drew closer to the pond, Judy noticed an overhung branch used for diving, a raft floating a little further out and the path that led to the falls. The men had waited for their arrival before disturbing the quietness of the pool, but it was now full of ripples and waves from their activity.

Judy waited her turn to dive. She decided that was the best way to make her first plunge. When her turn came, she walked out on the branch, not aware of the picture she made with her multi-color suit, poised on the branch like an exotic bird ready for flight. She pushed off the branch, throwing her body out and then down into the water with a graceful dive. She surfaced immediately to a round of applause. They stayed in the pool for over an hour with games and fun, Judy was exhausted and ready to call it a night. She was so relaxed and all the days tension had been erased with the cool waters massaging her tired, stiff muscles.

Judy slipped out of the water and went behind a huge tree to slip on her clothes; she was not going to give Ben anything else to criticize her on if she could prevent it. She climbed into the back and was lazing back waiting for the two men to leave. She must have dozed off, because when she opened her eyes, they were in front of her trailer.

Chapter 20

The next few days flew by. The roads were completed, the trenches dug for the pipes, and the foundation for the plant was finished. Tony was a man of his word. The trucks with supplies and tools were arriving daily and best of all she had completed all the necessary drawings and specks for starting to build. When possible she had stayed out of Ben's way and things were going smooth.

It was almost the end of her second week on the job. She was relaxed and had a feeling of finally belonging . It was close to noon, the sun was high overhead and even with the air conditioner going full force, it was hot and humid in the work trailer. Judy decided as many mistakes as she was making; she would do better if she waited for evening, when it cooled off some.

It had become a habit of hers to set a gallon jar out for sun tea every morning, as she picked up the jar it was so hot she flinched. It was hard to believe it could become so hot in such a short time. She showered and changed to a cool sundress before making some sandwiches. She had just made a large pitcher of ice tea when she heard Mike and Ben come in for their lunch. She went across with her arms full of sandwiches and the container of ice tea.

"If someone will open the door, the reward will be worth it!"

Ben appeared almost immediately from inside to open the door. Judy realized the minute it was out, she had said the wrong thing, her face turned scarlet. Ben must have sensed her embarrassment.

He smiled as he opened the door. "Lady, you are an angel from heaven. I think those dam trucks arrived on the hottest day we have ever had. We stopped work until the sun goes down, otherwise someone will have a heat stroke."

Ben reached for the ice tea as he yelled toward the back of the trailer. "Mike! We have company. Come out decent."

"You'll have to excuse the way I look. I lost the toss for the shower. I always do, I don't know why I even bother. It is a good thing I am not a gambler, I always come in second best."

"You could look at it as a win, you get first choice at the sandwiches and tea. Some people would choose food over cleanness."

"I could also consider it a win because I get more time alone with a beautiful lady, who looks so cool and refreshing herself, it is hard to take my eyes off her."

"I hope it isn't too scant, I really don't want to be any trouble, it is so hot and clothes just cling to my skin. I don't think I have ever been so uncomfortable."

"Judy, you are allowed to be a lady. It is not too scant, you are not the type to flaunt your femininity, I said some very negative things when you first came so please forgive me and believe me when I say you are being more than considerate of the situation with the men. I don't think a one of them would get out of line with you. They have learned to respect you. I just hope you don't feel it necessary to keep avoiding me."

Judy was surprised at Ben's remark. It had become more and more difficult avoiding him and it must have been obvious, not only to him but the others as well. Mike came into the room in shorts and loose shirt, his hair still wet from the shower.

"I thought Ben was pulling my leg so he could get me out of the shower sooner, what a pleasant surprise. This is great of you Judy. We are about as hungry as we are hot."

"I'm getting a shower before I eat guys, I will have another glass of that tea to take with me while I clean up though. You two don't wait, go ahead with the sandwiches, just save me some."

Ben filled his glass and with a smile, thanked Judy again for her thoughtfulness.

Judy and Mike had taken their time and were just sitting down to eat when Ben returned. They all ate and talked over the progress so far when Ben looked at Mike and said, "Do you want to tell Judy what the plans are or do I?"

"You are head man, You can have the honors."

Judy had a feeling they were trying to avoid an issue somehow, It made her uneasy not knowing what to expect.

Ben leaned back in his chair and looked at Judy, "Carl and I are leaving tomorrow and will be gone a few days,

The other job we were on is now complete. Only a few loose ends to tie up and we will be pulling the last of our crew out. That's where we were the day you arrived, which brings us to the problem. There are several more men and two with families coming from that job to work here. You have worked your buns off on the plans and Mike, Carl and I feel we have enough to start on right away. We don't want to pressure you if you feel you need more time, we will hold off, but we must pull the men out of where they are and settle them in here within the week. We will fly some into Manaus for rest and relaxation for a few days but all the equipment and personal belongings will be brought here and the men all settled in first."

"Where are we going to put all of them?

Are there more mobile homes?'

"Unfortunately no. We will have to double up and make do until some of the living quarters are completed. Millie and Carl will take Jack, Lonny and their two little ones. The single men can double up enough to make do temporally, which leaves us to one last little family of three. A new baby of only six months old does not fit into Mike and my lifestyle, so…. We thought…. If you trust us enough to move into our spare bedroom, we can put them in your trailer. I know it is an imposition and we won't be mad if you say no, but we really prefer your company to the other option. We will give you your own bathroom. Mike and I will share the other one. Your room will be to the back, away from us, so you will not hear our snoring. What do you say?"

"With such an embellished invitation, how could I refuse? Of course I'll move in here. It isn't much different than a rooming house I once stayed in; I even shared a bathroom with a man there.

I don't see why we can't start on some of the homes. Carl has the land all cleared and as soon as he gets back we can mark the ground for the foundation. The supplies seem to be coming form Tony well enough to keep us going. We can mark the foundation and things are progressing so well with the plant, he said we can split the crew.

I have about got the final list of materials ready. I can stay ahead of them without too much pressure. I do want to be on the job site as much as possible so if we could move the work trailer down there it would make it a lot easier for me. Other than that, I see no Problems."

Ben nodded his head as he said, "After we get the plant built, It won't take them long to get some of the homes livable. By splitting the worker and work on both projects we will need to make sure the supplies are here. With the government supplying the materials, I need to get your list to Tony as soon as possible so he can start on his end.

Mike you will help Judy move and see that the work-trailer gets moved for her. As soon you get things organized, you can make a trip to town for anything we might need and deliver Judy's list to Tony. You and Millie know what is needed, so have her start a list. Looks like we are ready to make things happen around here. There won't be much time for anything but work once we get going. One thing Judy, I must stress, you are not to go anywhere alone while we are gone, even though you have a guard following you. You either have Carl or one of the other managers with you at all times. That goes for all the women, they are to stay close to camp and keep the kids close. We have had some recent sittings of possible trouble in the area, so everyone be on alert.

Chapter 21

The sun was dropping behind the trees and it was cooling a little by the time they were through discussing the plans.

Ben and Mike went off to check on things that need to be done. This left Judy to herself again to work.

She finally felt like she was a part of things. Ben had included her in the planning and never even questioned her statements, but excepted them openly.

She realized she had been working for some time, but had no idea what time it was when she heard Millie yelling for her. Judy jumped and ran to the door. Millie was standing on her porch waving to her.

"Close up shop and come over. I need your help."

Judy laughed as she turned to close up the work trailer. Leave it to Millie to see that she didn't overwork, she thought. She was sure Millie was anxious to hear how she felt about the changes. It was going to be hard. She would take a six-month-old baby to bunk with opposed to Ben, but her little trailer only had one bed. Even for the couple and a baby, it would be cramped.

When she suggested the work trailer, she was told two of the men would be bunking in there temporarily, but they would be gone before she went to work and would be eating lunch with the others. It wasn't going to be easy for any of them, so she would just make the best of a necessary situation she thought as she walked across to see how Millie was preparing for the onslaught of company.

As Judy stepped out into to hot sun she was sure she heard footsteps in the jungle behind the trailer, the hair at the back of neck bristled as she hurried across the opening to Millie's trailer. It could have been an animal but Judy had the feeling someone had been out back checking on who was in the trailer. Where was the guard? Judy turned and saw him coming from the opposite direction of where she had heard the movement.

She stopped him and told him what she heard and he went to check it out as Judy continued on to visit with Millie. "Judy, you work too hard."

"I know Millie, but I have to get finished with the housing so we can get the waste and energy plant started, besides, you don't want permanent house guests do you?"

"You know Carl and I never had any children of our own, so when Jack brought Lonnie down as a new bride six years ago, we sort of adopted them. They are like family. This is their last year in the field. The kids will be school age; they're transferring back home. We sure will miss them. I never figured Lonnie would stay, but she did and she has been a good wife and mother. Never complains always supports Jack in anything he decides to do. You'll like her.

The kids too. They are good and love Brazil, but they need to be with other youngster's their own age.

"It must be hard raising children so far away from home and family."

"It is. We all go home around the holidays. It rains so much that time of year; they decided it was best to just close down for two or three weeks. Some of the local workers see to keeping a path through the forest while we are away. Some stay away a month. This is home to us so two weeks is all we care about. I almost forgot what I called you across for. I am making homemade ice cream for Mike's birthday and need two extra hands."

"I have never made ice cream, but just tell me what I can do. I can't imagine having to make something like ice cream. There are so many things we take for granite at home because it is so readily available. What do we do first?"

"The custard is heating on the stove. All's in it is eggs, sugar, milk and Junket."

"I wondered what Junket was when we filled the orders back home."

Millie brought the creamy mixture out on the porch where she had a tub sitting. Inside the tub, was a tall wood keg. She poured the creamy mixture in a steel container in the keg, then placed a long beater with wood paddles on it inside the can containing the creamy mixture. The lid had a hole in the middle so the stem of the beater came out to attach to a gear mechanism, so when the handle turned, it caused the beaters to rotate in the cream. This was Judy's job, turning the handle.

"Now you turn that handle, not fast but steady and don't stop. I will put the ice around the can in the keg. Keep It moving now."

Judy did as Millie instructed and watched as she chipped the ice in small piece to fit in the keg around the can, adding rock salt as she filled the keg. When the keg was filled and overflowing with ice and rock salt, Millie took over the turning for a while to give Judy a rest. When Judy saw Millie laboring over cranking the handle, she took I back. It was getting hard to turn and they both were tired when Carl arrived. He relieved the ladies and started turning the handle with little effort. Millie insisted Judy eat with them and was busy in the kitchen now that Carl had rescued her from the ice cream making. Judy stayed with Carl and made sure there was always ice around the can.

"Judy, you can go get Millie, tell her it is time to pack it down."

Millie had heard Carl and was coming out the door with a big bowl and wooden spoon. Mike and Ben arrived and took over helping. Mike removed enough ice to get the top off. As Mike pulled the paddles out Millie used the wooden spoon to scrape the ice cream off it. After they got the beater out, Mike closed up the can, sealed the hole with a cork and packed ice around and on top of the can to let it set while they ate dinner.

The other workers came up for dessert. Millie helped Mike cut the cake while Judy and Carl unpacked the ice cream. Ben sat smoking his pipe, watching. When everyone was served, Judy sat down with her own bowl. It was the most delicious ice cream she had ever eaten. Everyone ate until they couldn't eat anymore. The hand freezer made five gallons of ice cream, so there was plenty left. Judy helped Millie store the remainder in the freezer. It was almost midnight before the little party broke up and everyone went off to bed.

CHAPTER 22

The next morning Ben and Carl were gone when Judy started across to work. Mike waved as he left with the men. It was almost lunchtime when Mike and the men returned to move the work trailer. Judy had brought a small drafting board with her but with the big ones in the work trailer she had not used it. She decided to set it up at one end of the trailer she would be sharing with Mike and Ben, that way she still could work late without disturbing the men in the work trailer.

She worked the next few days diligently and was settled in Ben and Mike's trailer. Her little trailer was clean and ready for its new tenants.

Ben and Carl had been gone five days, Mike had turned in but Judy still sat working at the drafting table. She heard the screen door open and looked up just as Ben walked in the door. "What the hell are you doing working at this time of night?"

Judy stretched her arms out and pivoted her neck to relieve the stiffness from sitting in one position for hours. Her neck muscles were tight and ached. Ignoring Ben's remark she said, "Oh Wow! I guess time got away from me. Is it late?"

Ben walked over to her and gently turned her so her back was to him and started massaging her neck and shoulders. She relaxed and let her head fall forward. It felt so good. His hands were strong and the massaging had a hypnotic effect. She could feel the tightness leaving her aching muscles. After a few minutes the massaging became a slow caressing sensation. Judy slowly drifted into a dream like mood. "How's that, feel better?" Ben was so close, when he spoke, his warm breath brushed her neck, making her tremble.

He must have misread her reaction. He immediately dropped his hands and stepped back. "Go to bed Judy, its after midnight. You won't be fit to live with tomorrow if you don't get your beauty sleep."

He turned and was gone before she could even respond or thank him. What had happened? Judy was still trying to figure out Ben's actions an hour later. Sleep just wouldn't come. She regretted the reaction his warm breath had caused, she felt if she had just said something right away maybe it would have been ok, but she was so shocked at her own action, she couldn't speak. She had never been so affected by a man breathing on her neck. Lord knows it wasn't the first time it had happened. On every job there was always at least one jerk that thought he was irresistible to every woman. He must have thought she was scared or upset by his actions. That was the only reason she could imagine. So how was she to let him know otherwise, without sounding downright stupid? ""Oh, by the way, you didn't upset me last night, I was just overcome with emotions." No, it would just have to pass for now. Judy drifted off to sleep still in a ponder over the encounter.

Chapter 23

Judy woke to the sound of heavy equipment and engines of all sorts. She glanced at her bedside clock. It was pass ten o'clock. She must have forgot to set her alarm. She jumped out of bed and ran for the shower. I am sure I turned it on, I must have turned it off in my sleep.

Less than thirty minutes later she was out the door and looking around to see what was happening.

Mike was the first to spot her, "Hi Sleepyhead, you feel better after a decent rest? Ben said you were still working after midnight when he came in, so he turned your alarm off."

Ben came in while I was sleeping. "I feel fine," she said to Mike, "What does he want me to do? Any orders or am I on my own?"

"He said if you were up before noon, I was to bring you over to the building site. He and Carl are marking it off for foundations and could use your expert advice. Jump aboard I'll give you a ride."

"Only if I get to drive."

Mike was on a big tractor that had been brought over from the other job and was clearing away more brush around the back of all the trailers. "You got it. Ever driven one of these?"

"A few times."

As they headed for the area where they were to start work, Mike said, "Things grow so fast, we are constantly working to clear the ground. You can almost see it grow. Soon the rains will start. We will get rain every night. It starts around ten and rains for at least two hours.

"Mike, was Ben upset or mad with me? I mean did he say anything about last night?"

"No, he just seemed concerned, he thinks you are pushing yourself too hard."

Judy did not say anything else, she didn't know what else to say. Here she was thinking Ben was going to be mad at her and instead he was being very considerate of her. Dam him, why was he so hard to understand.

Carl and Ben were looking over her drawings as she and Mike arrived.

Carl came over and helped her down as soon as she as she came to a stop and shut down the engine. "Nice piece of driving. Just in time. We have the lines ready to string. You take the plans and lead us to the one you want first. We will pull the lines and get them pegged so the crews can start first thing in the morning. Mike and I will work this side, you and Ben work the other side."

"You can see why Carl is so good at his job. He even bosses the boss," Mike said as he took the plans from him, "better do what he says Judy, it is easier than trying to argue with him."

They were all laughing as Mike started walking away with the drawings.

Judy said, "we don't need those," indicating the plans he carried, "I can walk it off blindfolded." She had built this little city in her mind a hundred times already.

As she pegged a spot for Mike and Carl to start from, she walked across what would be a street one-day and started lining up the other side for Ben.

"You want to put the pegs in or go work the tripod?" she ask Ben.

"Your little nap rejuvenated you I see. You were pretty tired last night," then turned and in a louder voice, "I'll peg you tell me where. We'll see who can finish first."

They worked at it steady and had just finished marking the last one. Ben looked across and laughed as he yelled to Mike and Carl. "You two need some help? We already finished with our side."

"It wasn't fair, you had the expert helping you. It was a struggle just to get this far. Carl is about ready to pound me instead of the peg. You two worked good together."

"We make a good team, we'll have a rematch sometime, you call the time and place next time." Ben was saying as he and Judy went across to help finish the other side.

It didn't take long to finish and they all went into the work trailer to cool off and plan the next few days work schedule.

Most of the men were working on the Waste to Energy plant. It had to be finished before they could move anyone into the homes. As soon as it was well under way, some of the men would work on the housing. Having the plans for the plant almost completed before she came down was a big help.

"We have the building walls almost finished on the plant site and it won't take long to get it ready for the equipment inside. Have you designed one of these plants before Judy," Mike was asking. "It sure looks like you have. It is a big project."

"Yes Mike, I did one for the last place I worked. It was built in Canada; I was there about three months. I had the plans drawn and the materials ordered out before I went up. It's a great way to go for remote areas. We will have all the electricity we need, the sewage and waste will be disposed of properly. After the plant is finished, we will have only the guesthouse to build. If we don't run into too much trouble or the rain doesn't stop us too much, we should be through in less than the year as guaranteed."

Ben had lit his pipe and was listening to them talk, but he never ask her any questions.

He finally spoke, "We better get back and get some rest. Mike, remember, you are flying over for supplies tomorrow. You will want to be up early. Judy, if you have the list of materials and equipment finished, give it to Mike. He can drop by the government office and get things rolling on that end. We have enough lumber to start the foundations, but the machinery will have to be brought in. I just hope we don't have any problems getting everything you need."

By the time they returned to the living quarters, the sun was going down and it was a little cooler. Judy had showered and in the kitchen when Ben walked in. His hair was still damp and he had shaved. "You must have won the toss for first shower tonight."

"Nah, Mike just took pity on me for a change. What are we going to eat?"

"I opened a canned ham and sliced some. That's as far as I got. I am too tired to do too much. I sure miss my fresh salads."

"Tell Mike, he can bring some back tomorrow. We all could do with some fresh vegetables and fruit. We will grow our own once everything gets going and get settled into a regular routine. Lonnie had a great garden she left behind at the last job."

"Judy could come with me," Mike said as he strolled in the kitchen.

"No, she has too much to do right now. I am taking her tomorrow to check on things at the plant. It is important to get that plant built so we won't be slowed down when the rains come. Once it's closed in we can work on the inside operations of the plant. I also would like some of the homes completed before the rains come, specially one for Carl and Millie before we go home for our break. You know they stay here most of the time.

You could take Millie if she wants to go. It might be good for her to do the shopping for food instead of you."

So much for being included in the plans. Judy couldn't help from saying, "Why didn't you tell me what you had planned? I am a person you know and I like to know what is going on without getting it indirectly."

"I intended to at dinner. The situation arose sooner, that's all. Don't make more out of it than there is to it. I think we should concentrate on getting that plant up and running. I don't feel the plant is safe for you be work on alone right now, not until we have more of our men on the site. It is too isolated and Mike will tell you, we do have some problems with the locals. You are too sensitive Judy. Don't let it become a problem.

What was his problem, Judy thought, he probably hates women in general, why else bury yourself in the jungle for years. Judy knew that was unfair, Mike had been here as long and he was nice, no, it was just Ben and his temperament.

They had finished eating and were clearing the table when Mike said, "Judy you go work on the lists, we will do this."

Judy knew she should be concentrating on what was needed and not Ben, she didn't want to forget anything. Any small item could hold up progress for days once they got started.

"Thanks Mike, I guess I better go over it again. How long do you think it will take to get the material here?"

"One week usually. Tony seems to be pushing ours through pretty fast and if they fly most on the materials in we won't have to wait at all. The larger pieces of machinery for the plant will take a week by truck. It depends on who we get to work with. I will know more tomorrow after I meet with Tony."

Judy spent the rest of the evening at the drafting table. She was about to call it a night when Mike came up behind her. "Don't make another late night of it, Ben will be upset again. He seems to get upset with you to often. We need to see what we can do about that."

Judy rolled up a large sheet she had been working on and slipped it into a tube with some smaller papers. "Mike I made a sketch of what the whole project will look like on completion. I thought it might make your sales job a little easier if we could show what the finished product would look like." As she tapped his chest with the cardboard cylinder containing the papers, she said, "Take these. Good luck and good night!"

Mike took the papers, "Thanks Punkin, good night to you too. See you when I get back."

Ben was on the porch smoking, so she went off to bed without even a good night to him.

Chapter 24

Judy was awake and dressed before her alarm rang. She was rested and anxious to get started. Ben and Mike were fixing breakfast when she went out into the living area.

"Want an egg Judy?"

"Yuk! No! Can't stand the sight of an egg in the morning."

Mike laughed, "What do you survive on? With all that go power, you must eat something."

"I like cereals, toast and juice. I have been known to eat left over Pizza for breakfast. If I eat eggs, I have them in an omelet for dinner."

"The 'Unconventional Lady'! "Why doesn't that surprise me," Ben said, as he poured coffee in the three mugs she had sat on the counter. "The unusual is the norm for you it seems."

"I am not sure how to respond to that, so I'll let it pass."

"After eating and clearing the table, Ben said, "Leave the washing up, I have made arrangements for one of the women to do that for us. She is eager to have something to do to occupy her long days. She will prepare meals for us as well. It adds a few dollars to their income. The company will pay her."

"What a relief, I hate kitchen chores."

Laughing Ben again, "The 'Unconventional Lady' again. It's considered ladies work. You ready Mike? I'll see you off before Judy and I leave, I want to talk to Carl," Ben said as he headed for the door. "Is Millie going?"

"I don't know, I talked to her last night and she will let me know this morning. You know Millie and flying."

Their voices drifted out of Judy's hearing as she felt like throwing something at him.

When Ben returned, Judy was ready to go. She had stored all she need in a backpack and had it laying on the table. Ben had been in long pants so she dressed the same, her boots of course and a loose fitted kaki shirt.

When he returned his only comment was, "Lets go."

CHAPTER 25

The next few weeks flew by. Everyone was busy and had very little time off. Sundays were set aside for relaxing. Most everyone went to the swimming hole for the afternoon. They had picnic lunches there and sometimes made ice cream. They loaded the vehicles with food; drinks, ice and anything else needed for a relaxing afternoon. They all worked together for months and established binding friendships. Judy was accepted and included in all the groups but at the same time, being very careful not to get to friendly with any of the men. Judy had hired Marie to do her laundry while she was cooking and cleaning for them, so she had formed a friendship with her, but she was most comfortable with Millie and Lonny. She had become quite fond of Jack and Lonny's children. She played games with them and undertook teaching them to swim.

She recalled one particular afternoon where she was in the shallow water with Becky and Robby. Becky was holding around her neck from behind, as she was working with Robby and his swimming strokes. He had learned to stay afloat by thrashing and splashing so Judy was trying to teach him to relax and not fight the water. Ben came up behind her and took Becky from around her neck.

"You look like you could use some help. Becky is leaving a permanent mark on your neck. You are doing a good job with them. Robby will out swim us in another week."

The Weight of Becky being lifted off her was a big relief. She was tired, but did not want to exclude her while working with Robby.

"Thanks, I appreciate the help."

Becky was squealing and laughing in delight as Ben pulled her rapidly through the water with strong arms. It took very little effort on his part as Judy watched the muscles in his upper arm flex with each move. She tried to concentrate on Robby and his swim strokes until he showed sign of disinterest. She gave up and they all started splashing and playing. They were getting exhausted when Ben suggested some cookies might revive them causing a scramble for shore.

Judy was heading in also when she felt a hand on her shoulder. She turned around, Ben was close, "Let them go, let's swim out to the raft for a rest."

Ben swam beside her in easy gliding stokes all the way, "I was afraid they had tired you too much to swim to the raft. You are a strong swimmer."

"I love swimming and was lifeguard two summers in college."

As they reached the raft, she easily pulled up on it. Some of the others were there. They all relaxed and did very little talking. It had been an enjoyable afternoon.

CHAPTER 26

The telephones had been connected as Tony had promised, and they were in contact with the government offices regularly. Tony had talked to Judy on several occasions, each time stressing his desire to see her. She would enjoy getting away for a day and see some of Brazil other than jungle. She knew, however, the least encouragement on her part could cause Tony to pursue her even more, so each time she declined the invitation, saying they were too busy.

Mike had overheard her conversation on one occasion and commented on Tony's persistence. "He likes you Judy, unless the feeling is mutual, be very careful. I will try and be around when he is here. He is not easily discouraged is he?"

"I don't encourage him Mike, I have no desire to, but I am trying to keep it strictly business with him. He could cause delays and give us some real problems."

"I know and I have no idea what type of man Tony is, I will tell Ben and Carl when I get a chance so they are aware of it also. You can't help being so dammed appealing 'Punkin'. Don't worry, we will see it through."

It was on Tuesday morning when Ben first mentioned a weekend in town. Millie was keeping Becky and Robby so Jack and Lonny could go along. Judy knew Ben had arranged it for her benefit. She and Lonny had become good friends and while the men attended a meeting at the government office, she and Lonny were to have a day of shopping and relaxing, doing whatever women enjoyed doing he had said.

The rest of the week was filled with planning and excitement. The children were in Judy's bedroom helping her decide what to pack while Lonny watched.

"You have some beautiful clothes Judy. I am getting anxious to go home so I can dress in fashionable clothes again. I love Jack and whatever he decides to do I will go along with him, but it would be nice to live like others for a while." She hesitated for a few minutes before continuing, "What about you Judy, are you willing to stay longer than your year if things get more serious with you and Ben?"

Judy turned and looked at Lonny, "What do you mean?"

"I have eyes, Judy, Millie and I see how he looks after you. Ben has never show any interest in a woman before, so it is easy to read a loaner. We like you both and we don't want either to get hurt. Be careful, living like this takes a special type of person. I have seen several come and go. It is not an easy way to live and it takes total commitment on both sides. Believe me, I know."

"I don't know, I feel like I could stay forever right now. The only thing that would make me want to leave is if I couldn't do my job well enough. I don't want to fail all of you, but after this job is done, who knows. It is too soon to tell. I don't think Ben will ever want me enough to ask me to stay. I think his interests are just male admiration or male instincts to protect. Let's see how things are in another few months, right now let's concentrates on having a fun weekend.

As she spoke she picked up a beautiful pink floral dress and tossed it to Lonny, "Here try this on. I have no idea why I ever bought it. It is not my color and it will look great on you."

Lonny laughed as picked up the exquisite designer dress, "Judy it is lovely, but I can't take it. It must have cost a fortune."

"Nonsense, it's yours. What do you say kids, do you think Mommy should have a pretty dress to wear to town?"

They both jumped up and down yelling, "Yes! Yes! Yes!"

"See you are outnumbered, It's yours. You and Millie can fit it tomorrow if it needs it."

"Thank you Judy, I love it." She gathered the dress to her, "Come on children, time to get ready for bed. Tell Judy good night."

It was too quite after they left, Judy finished her packing and went out in the other room to get a cold drink. She filled her glass with ice tea and headed for the porch. It was dark, but she sensed someone presence. She glanced in the corner where she saw a shadow. It was Ben, leaning against the corner post, with his pipe in his mouth.

"Well, did you get everything packed. I could hear the kids and Lonny all the way across to their place talking about the dress you gave her."

"I don't know who is more excited about this trip, the kids, or Lonny and I. We have changed our minds several times on what clothes to take and what we want to do.

"I think Lonny would like to just spend the day shopping and being a woman. She hasn't had anyone to go with in the past and now she is getting nervous about returning home as well. She had been home on visits, but most of her last five years have been here in the jungle, where a woman is more concerned about comfort and not style."

"Yes, she mentioned that earlier. She'll adjust fast. She and the children will be fine. How will Jack take to the changed? It is really going to be hard on him. Everything at home is so different. I just hope it all works out for them."

"I am sorry I put off a trip to town so long, Judy. We were so busy and when everything is going well, we men fail to think of anything else."

Aloud clash of thunder shook around them as the sky light up with lightening. "It's going to pour down rain any minute. The wind is cooling things off a little. Do the storms still upset you?"

"I have learned to live with it. I have even got use to torrential rains."

"Have you Judy? I was just going to warn you we are in for a big storm. Like the one when you first arrived. Come over here and stand in front of me, you can see it coming over the hills. There is a break in the trees where you can see it approaching."

Ben pulled her over in front of him and let his hands rest on her shoulders. She could see the lighting way off in the hills, but as Ben said, it was moving towards them fast.

Ben left his hands on her shoulder; she could feel the warmth of them as she stood watching the storm get closer and closer. She couldn't tell if she swayed or if he pulled her back so she was leaning against his hard body. She leaned into him as his hands slid down her arms and closed around her wrists, crossing them in front of her and holding her there. It was so pleasant. They stayed that way a long time, watching as the storm moved in their direction.

"We are going to get wet if we stay here much longer. You remember how quickly the other one was on us? It's late you should go in. You need all the rest you can get for that shopping trip Saturday."

He turned her around. Judy let her head fall back so she could look into Ben's face as it closed in on her. His kiss at first was soft and sensuous, but as he drew her closer to him it was as though he was becoming part of her. Judy felt her bones would crush under Ben's masculine hold on her. She too was clutching him, wanting him to not let her go. Ben finally pulled away slightly. Judy felt weak and dazed. She still held onto his shoulders, letting her head fall into the hollow of his neck, she felt his lips brush against the top of her head as the sky lit up and a crash of thunder brought them back to reality. They sprang for the door at the same time.

"Good Night Judy!" Ben turned her and gave her a shove in the direction of her bedroom. The emphatic 'good night' told her he was thankful for the storm, but the smile on his face gave her hope.

Judy didn't go to sleep right away. As she lay listening to the storm building up force outside, she again was at odds with herself. Lonny had brought up a good point. Did she want to continue to work in the foreign field to be with Ben if it came to that or could she walk away at the end of the year and not look back? It would not be fair to Ben to go into it with that in mind either. If he really cared for her and at the end of the project, she went home, what effect would it have on him. By the time sleep came she was no closer to an answer than she was when he had pushed her away. There was only one thing she was sure of; she was falling in loved with Ben. If she weren't careful, she would be the one with a broken heart.

Chapter 27

The weather had cleared by Friday. Judy and Lonnie were putting their luggage on the plane for an early start on Saturday. Lonny was having second thoughts about leaving the children. She had never been away from them overnight.

Saturday the five were boarding the plane at sunup. Lonny was crying because Becky had woke up when she left and didn't want her to leave. Everyone finally convinced her the kids would survive under Millie's loving care as they boarded the plane. Judy had volunteered to pilot and Ben announced he would co-pilot.

"It will be good experience for you Judy. You may be required to fly alone someday and we wouldn't want you to get lost over the jungle. We are over a thousand miles inland and almost five hundred miles from Manaus. There is very few places to put down a plane and most roads are hidden from sight by trees and vines."

Judy shivered, "It is a little frightening, beautiful, but frightening. It is easy to understand how people can get lost forever in this country."

They talked and laughed until the city came into view. They circled the city for a good view. It was a magnificent sight. The city sitting on the edge of the massive Amazon River and the jungle surrounding the three other sides as though it were just waiting to reclaim the land. Unfortunately the Jungle always loses to progress and civilization.

Judy was talking to the tower and getting her landing instructions.

"Do you want me to take her in Judy?"

"No way, I want to."

Ben smiled and nodded his head. Everyone else was quiet while Judy landed and taxied the plane to a smooth stop.

"Great job Judy. If I didn't like you so much I would be jealous of all your talents. Is there anything you can't do?"

"Thanks Lonny, I could say the same thing about you, with those precious children."

"That's no talent Honey, just a good choice of man."

They all laughed, Ben looked at Judy, she knew her face flushed, as he gave her a knowing grin.

Ben had made arrangements for a car to be waiting for them. It was at their disposal while in Manaus. Mike was driving, Ben was in the front with him. He turned halfway around so he could see while talking to the three in the back seat. "We will check in at the hotel and get settled. Jack, I think it best you accompany the ladies on their shopping spree, while Mike and I take care of business. We should be back at the hotel by three or four. We'll be at the pool if we are not in our rooms when you get back. We can all have dinner and decide what to do for the evening. I will act as tour guide tomorrow for sightseeing if anyone is interested. Judy was interested in the tour, but Lonny and Jack were not sure yet.

"If its alright with you Ben, I would like to skip dinner and make other plans."

"Sure Mike, take the car, we will use taxies for whatever we decide."

"Thanks Ben."

No one questioned Mike or said anything about his other plans, but Judy was curious as to the nature of it. She suspected it was a woman, but it was unusual that he had not mentioned anyone in all their talking. She also got the impression Ben knew, but he was not volunteering any information either. Judy wondered if it was a woman, what type of woman Mike found appealing. It would be interesting to meet the mysterious woman.

The remainder of the trip to the hotel, everyone took turns calling Judy's attention to points of interest. The Portuguese explorers founded Manaus; it rose to prominence in the late nineteenth century by exporting rubber to the world. At the time the Amazon region was the only place on the globe where rubber trees could be found. But over the years synthetic rubber development and seeds were smuggled to start growth of rubber elsewhere. Manaus almost vanished. In 1967 the government declared it an international free trade zone and helped restore the city. Today it is a thriving city with over a million people. Mike and Ben supplied most of the information, while the other three listened with interest.

"There are many new roads being cleared through the jungle, one comes within twenty miles of our camp." Ben was speaking, "It is the one our trucks come on with our supplies. It is usually a three or four day drive to the turn off to our area, but from there the trucks have a rough time getting through with dirt road, which sometimes are overgrown and hard to travel as well as being threatened at times with bandits. When we have heavy storms like the one this week they have to go slow because of mud and downed trees in the way.

Mike pulled into a curved driveway, covered from the elements, and came to a stop in front of a luxurious hotel.

While smiling, Ben stated, "Stewart has a contract with this hotel for our visits. The rooms are paid for by Hardell International, but any other expenses are your own."

They all got out, Lonny and Judy waited just inside where it was cool while the men arranged for the luggage to be brought in. At the desk, Judy registered with the others. She was surprised to see they all had separate rooms, except Jack and Lonny of course. When they went up, they all got off at the same floor. Her room was next to Jack and Lonny's, Ben's was next, them Mike next to Ben.

Judy unlocked her room and entered. It was larger than she expected and the bed was king-size. The pale yellow spread with white trim looked fresh and cool. A comfortable chair in the same cool print sat in one corner by a dark wood desk. The French doors, covered with white sheers and draped with the yellow print as well, opened onto a veranda. The veranda had gates to access the joining ones.

Judy quickly unpacked and was storing her luggage when she heard a soft knock on the door.

"Ben and Mike left for their meeting. We're ready any time you are."

"I'll get my purse, I'm ready."

There was a huge Mall near the hotel. They first found a nice restaurant for lunch, then shopped until they were exhausted. They were loaded down with packages and were heading back to the hotel. Jack had been great, he left them as soon as they were in the store and magically reappeared to relieve them of their packages when they were ready to go to another store.

There were so many beautiful bright print cottons to choose from, Judy bought several. They were loose fitting so they would be cool, much more appropriate for the climate than the ones she brought. Brazil manufactured beautiful leather shoes and shoes being one of Judy's weaknesses, she bought two pair of sandals and pair of pretty dresses shoes.

Both she and Lonny bought for Millie and Carl, and of course, they bought for the children, so by the time they headed back to the hotel, all three were loaded with packages. They were making their way across the lobby when Mike and Ben came in the front door, reliving the ladies of some of their packages, they all entered the elevator, "You Must have bought the stores out." Ben juggled packages to push the elevator button. We will help you take your purchases up, then we have all been invited to have a drink with Tony. He is parking his car and will meet us in the lounge. He wants to take us to dinner."

Judy looked at Mike. He winked and smiled; "It will be alright Punkin."

Judy wasn't too sure of that. Mike had promised to protect her from Tony and he was not going to be there. She was not looking forward to this evening at all.

Mike was true to his word. In the lounge when they went down to meet Tony for a drink, he took her by the elbow and pulled her in beside him, sliding across the back seat as Ben slid in on the other side of her. Lonny sat across from Judy, between Jack and Tony. Judy could see Lonny was trying to suppress a laugh, when she glanced at her. Ben got up to help Tony with the tray of drinks, giving Judy a chance to kick Lonny under the table and caution her to not laugh.

Judy turned to Mike, "Traitor, you told everyone didn't you?"

"Yes, Mike told us about Tony. Everything will be fine tonight. We won't be rude to him, but we will help Ben."

The men were returning with the tray of drinks so they could not say anything else.

They had their drinks and made plans to meet in the lobby just before eight for dinner. After dinner, Tony had made plans to take them to some nightspots to dance. While the men had a second drink, the women decided they preferred a swim instead of another drink. They ask to be excused and left the men to themselves.

The elevator had not quite closed when Lonny looked at Judy, "What gives lady?"

"Lonny, I am having a terrible time keeping Tony at arms-length. He is so persistent. I like him, but not in that way. I only want to stay on friendly bases and not have it affect our work."

"Honey, even for you, Mike will not give up tonight. He has a beautiful lady he is pursuing, South America style. She comes from a very old Brazilian family."

They were standing outside Lonny's door, "I'll see you in a few minutes.

Come to my room when you are ready Judy. We can talk down by the pool."

Judy nodded her head and walked on to her room, thinking about what Lonny had just told her. It was odd that Mike had not mentioned anything about a woman to her. They had become close she had thought, but evidently not close enough. Judy undressed and put on her swimsuit, grabbed a cover-up on her way out the door. She rapped three times on Lonny's door.

Jack startled her as she ask, "What are you doing here, you are suppose to be drinking with the guys?"

"I chose to escort two beautiful ladies to the pool rather than drink. I hope that is ok with you."

"I'm sorry, I had my mind on something else. You surprised me when you opened the door is all. You must think I'm nuts?"

Lonny walked in from the bedroom, "What is going on? Are you two ready?"

"Ready and waiting, Honey, as always."

They were laying beside the pool on chase lounges after a swim. "It is so nice here isn't it? I get so little time away from the children but you know I feel guilty leaving them and can't help thinking about them. Do you think they will have a hard time adjusting to real life Judy?"

"I don't think so, it is not like they're being raised native or without guidance like Tarzan. They are intelligent children Lonny. They are eager to learn and they follow instructions from me. I would not worry if I were you. Put them in a preschool for a few months before school starts so they know what to expect."

"You are too serious for a vacation. "Jack pulled Lonny to her feet, "Let's go in swimming."

Judy was swimming a slow easy stroke across the deep end of the pool when a black head surfaced in front of her. She stopped swimming and tread water to keep from swimming into Ben. Her head bobbled above the water, looking into those ice blue eyes. "Trying to avoid us?"

"Not us, but one man in particular who can't take a hint." "That's good to know," he said as he turned and was gone before Judy could blink. He shot away like a fish under water, not even making a ripple as he went.

Judy didn't talk to Ben again. They stayed around the pool until it was time to go to their rooms to dress for dinner. The men played rough water games while she and Lonny set around in the shallow end talking.

Judy was dressed and contemplating going to Jack and Lonny's room when she heard a soft knock on her door. When she opened it, Ben's tall frame filled the opening. Judy had not seen him in a suit. She stood for a minute; he was one of the most handsome figures she had ever seen. In a dark navy suit with a light blue shirt he caught her off guard. She stood staring until he bowed slightly and handed her a small white flower.

"For you."

She finally came to her senses, "Thank you Ben, it's beautiful."

"I figured white would go with whatever you were wearing. You can wear it on your wrist if you want."

Judy was dressed in blue-green chiffon, which came to a low 'v' in front where the material crossed over starting at the waist. It flaring out as it covered her full bust, then narrowing at the shoulders where it was gathered with rhinestone bar pins the same color as the dress. The rhinestones reflected light when she moved, sparkling like diamonds. The dress had the same cross over in the back as the front, except it came much lower, exposing her soft white skin. She had pulled her hair up and away from her face, making her eyes look larger and brighter.

"It is going to be difficult keeping our friend at bay, you are beautiful in that dress."

"Do we have to go with Tony tonight?"

"Judy I tried, but without being rude, there was no way to avoid it. It will be alright."

The first person Judy saw when the elevator door opened was Tony. He was a very good-looking man and as he saw them, he waved and greeted them with a big smile. Mike and Lonny were already with them. As they walked across the lobby, Judy noticed the beautiful woman beside him. She was about Judy's age but there is where the comparisons ended. Any woman would kill for a complexion like hers, Judy thought. Her hair was raven black and her eyes were dark brown, almost black. Her perfectly fitted scarlet dress emphasized every sensuous curve of her body. She was one of the most beautiful women Judy had ever seen. She couldn't figure why Tony was showing so much interest in her, when he had someone as gorgeous as her.

"Ah! At last! We are all here. Ben, Judy, you must meet my cousin, Carla."

"Antonio, why must you insist on saying cousin? It is so far removed, it should not even be mentioned."

She then turned and addressed her remarks to Judy.

"I am so glad Antonio ask me to come. I was most anxious to meet you. He had told us very much about you. All of you," she said, as she let her eyes drift around the little group.

As Judy thanked her, she felt Ben's arm slide around her waist. He pulled her back so she was a little in front of him. She could feel the hard muscles of his thigh through the sheer material of her dress, causing her to shudder. Ben then circled her waist more, pulling her even closer, in a possessive way. She should not let it affect her. Ben was just trying to discourage Tony and make him think they were a pair, but her body reacted on its own. She could not control the sensation and Ben must have thought it was her actions toward Tony. As she glanced up he was smiling down at her as though they were the only two people in the lobby.

Tony raised a hand and motioned to the door as he said, "We must go, I made reservations for us. It is only a few minutes away. I am afraid we will be a little cramped. I hope the ladies pretty dresses do not get crushed."

As they approached Tony's car Ben said, "I'll sit in the back with the girls Jack, if you don't mind sitting in front?"

That's fine Ben, Lonny and I have been married long enough we don't mind being separated temporarily." They all laughed together, but Judy felt the two men were overdoing their protection thing a little.

The Maitre d' recognized Tony the minute they walked in. The restaurant was very elegant and they were seated at a table close to the dance floor, but far enough away from the music to converse easily. It was obvious Tony was well known and Judy had a feeling he wanted them to be aware of it.

Although Tony tried to seat her next to him, again Ben tactfully ushered her to the opposite side of the round table, seating her between him and Jack. She sat across from Tony, who had Carla on one side and Lonny on the other. Lonny was chatting a mile a minute to him about his excellent selection of restaurant.

Judy looked around the room as the waiter poured wine for Tony to approve. Tony nodded and everyone was poured a glass of wine. The room was beautifully decorated. The colors were soft and the lighting from the huge crystal chandelier were dimmed so there was no glare. Some of the guests were in formal dress.

"This is a popular restaurant for dining before attending the theater. It is a shame I did not have more notice. You would have enjoyed the performance, maybe another time we can plan for the theater."

When he talked he looked at Judy as though it were a special invitation to her. She sipped her wine and did not say anything. The conversation around the table was light and friendly

They had ordered their dinner and were waiting for the first course. Ben was talking to Carla. Jack and Lonny got up to dance and as she looked up, Tony said, "Would you dance with me Judy?"

Judy opened her mouth to refuse, then thought better of it. Ben was so busy flirting with Carla she would have to hit him over the head to make him ask her to dance. She rose as an answer to Tony's request. It was a Latin tune and she confessed to not knowing how to dance to his country's dances.

"It is very simple, you can waltz of course?"

"Yes, I do."

"Then all you must learn if to move a little with the hips and sway with the music." He teased, "I will help you."

Judy could see Ben still talking to Carla as though she was the only woman in the room. Tony had brought his cousin to distract Ben and the big lug was enjoying every minute of it. So much for his help, I might as well enjoy myself.

Judy followed Tony's lead and was having a good time. By the time the music ended she was flushed and laughing breathlessly when they returned to the table.

"You dance beautifully. We must try again later"

"Thank you, I enjoyed it, you are a good teacher."

Ben rose to seat her as she came around to her side of the table. If looks could kill, she would be dead. Why is he so mad, I couldn't refuse to dance with Tony? If he had not been so infatuated with Carla, he could have prevented it by dancing with her. Men, she thought, how in hell could you ever please one. He could flirt with Carla all he wants, she tried to convince herself, but I just don't want to appear like I am encouraging Tony. Insufferable male, Judy sat down and picked up her fork. She would like to have stuck Ben with it, instead she jabbed at the plate in front of her.

The dinner was very good. Judy had cooled down and was enjoying herself. They were all laughing and joking together by the time dinner was over. They were having a good time, but Judy was hoping they would make a short night of it.

She was about to suggest leaving when Ben turned to her, "Would you like to dance?"

She forgot she was suppose to be mad at him and accepted without hesitation.

It was a slow dance and as they approached the edge of the dance floor, Ben looked down at her, "You seem to enjoy your dance with Tony," as he pulled her to him, he said, "I'm not the dancer he is."

"You seem to be enjoying yourself without dancing. I am surprised you noticed, as I said before I don't want to encourage Tony, but by the same token, I can't be rude. He is nice and we have to work with him, but that is all."

They danced without talking until the music stopped. Ben was still holding her hand, not moving off the floor. As the music started again he turned her toward him, looking into her eyes, not saying a word he pulled her close into his arms. Resting his chin on her head, he let out a low groan as she tried to pull away to look at him, he held her so tight she could hardly breath. They barely moved as Ben held her close, while they slightly swayed to the music. She didn't realize until the music stopped that she was clinging to him just as tight, not wanting to let go.

Ben couldn't believe he was acting like such a jerk. It was as if he were a jealous teenager. This was a woman working for him and he was suppose to look out for her not let his emotions get out of control. He should not be feeling this way about her.

As they approached the table Lonnie tried to hide a yawn. Standing behind Jack and Lonnie, Ben showed no sign of setting, "We really should call it a night, we have a big day planned tomorrow. I am afraid we are not accustoming to late night entertainment Tony. I hope you don't think it rude and we don't want to spoil you evening, but I think the ladies are tired. It was very enjoyable. Thank you."

"I understand, I am sorry I did not realize it, I will see you back to the hotel."

"No, really, you and Carla stay if you want, we can take a taxi. It is only a few blocks. You have done enough."

Carla was not ready to leave and some friends had invited Tony and Carla to join them. Tony was standing as the four thanked them for their hospitality and said their good nights.

They were all quiet as the taxi made the short trip back to the hotel.

"I am bushed," Lonny half asleep on Jack's shoulder spoke, "I am just not use to all this, I have enjoyed it immensely Ben, I appreciate your inviting us."

"We hate to see your family leave, Jack is a good employee, and a good friend as well Lonny. I know your concerned for the children and the need for a normal life is your main reason for leaving, it is not a life for a man with ties. We are happy you stayed as long as you did."

They had arrived at the hotel and were waiting for the elevator as Ben addressed his answer to Lonnie but Judy felt Ben was sending a message to her as well. He did not want any responsibilities or ties.

Ben lightly touched her elbow as they entered the elevator but said nothing. As they passed Lonnie and Jack stopped in front of their door, Lonny said, "Let's meet on our terrace about nine o'clock for breakfast. We don't know yet if we want to go sightseeing or not."

"Fine, Judy and I will be ready." Judy was in front of her door when Ben answered. She smiled and said, "See you at nine then." He just nodded his head and continued on to his room. Judy was a little surprised, he didn't even say goodnight as he left her to open her own door.

CHAPTER 28

The next morning the sun shining through the French doors woke Judy early. She was dressed and ready to go long before nine o'clock, when she heard voices on the terrace next door and eager to be off, she went out. Lonnie and Jack were there as well as Ben.

"Here is our sleeping beauty." Lonny said as she passed Judy a cup of very strong coffee.

"I hope you're being dressed means you are coming with us." Judy didn't know if she could trust herself to be alone with Ben all day.

"We have decided to go. I am rested and Jack said we should see as much as possible since we may not get back down here until the kids are in college." Lonnie was laughing and talking as she served everyone from the lovely breakfast cart the hotel had prepared.

Lonnie and Judy were dressed in cool cotton dresses and sandals. They knew that by noon the heat would be unbearable. There was a car waiting for them when they went out of the hotel. Ben drove, Judy was in the front seat with him. As they drove through the town, Ben again was the spokesman.

"Manaus is a free port as I told you yesterday, so our profession, being what it is, I thought you might be interested in the floating dock built in the early 1900's by the British. It is capable of accommodating up to a forty-foot rise in the river during the rainy season. The Rio Negro, means Black Water, will join the muddy Amazon just below Manaus in what is known as 'Wedding of the Water'. The Rio Negro receives its dark color from leaves stewing in the eighty to ninety degree water, flowing from swamps in Colombia and Venezuela. You should have been able to see the joining of the river when you flew in from home Judy."

"I was asleep until just before landing unfortunately."

"We will make a point of flying over it when we go home for Christmas."

"I can't believe that is less than three months away. Time had gone so fast. I really enjoy working down here."

Ben turned his head and looked at Judy for as long as his driving would allow. She wasn't sure but Judy thought he started to say something them changed his mind.

The next stop is the Teatros Amazons, an ornate opera house built in 1896. This amazing theater was put together, piece by piece, with material entirely imported from Europe, paid for with taxes from the rubber exports. It was restored in 1974.

Judy and Ben were sitting admiring the many hues of blue-green and gold tiles in the theater. Lonnie and Jack were off somewhere at the moment, exploring on their own.

Ben took Judy by her arms and turned her where she was looking into those ice blue eyes that melted her heart. She had never let a man get close enough to do that before, but without warning, Ben had. From the very start, he had been able to touch her inner feelings. She had put a wall around her heart years ago in college when she was forced to make a choice between career and marriage. The other man was an engineer also and he wanted a wife not a partner, and to him, she couldn't be both. It hurt her deeply and she did not want it to happen again. She had learned to keep men at a distance until now. Ben's voice brought her back to today.

"Judy, we have to talk." Ben let her go and turned away. "I have tried to keep our relationship strictly business, but you know as well as I do, it has been difficult for both of us." Ben hesitated, choosing his words carefully. "This is no life for a married man. It is especially not for children. I like what I am doing and don't want to give it up. I can't get involved. It just would not work. I can't ask a woman to live the life I do." He turned to look at her again. His face reflecting hurt and despairs. "Do you understand what I am saying?"

Judy stared at Ben's face, trying not to blink her eyes. She felt tears welling up and knew if she blinked, tears would come, showing the hurt and disappointment. She lowered her head, looking at her hands. She cleared her throat before speaking.

"I think I do Ben. You are saying you have feelings for me but your job is more important. You seem to have decided already for both of us.

Judy had to get away from Ben. She needed time to get her emotions under control. She stood up and turned away to go, as she walked slowly out of the theater he called after her. She kept going increasing her speed with each step until she was running out the door. She found a shady place, outside, away from curious eyes. She would not let herself cry. Tears burned her eyes as she blinked them away, taking deep breaths until she finally had her emotions under control enough to face the others. She had let her guard down and now she again was in position to have her heart broken. She was so sure Ben cared for her and she had thought there might finally be someone for her. Someone who could share her work with and at the same time have a life. What difference did it make about the job and shouldn't they make the decision together, not him alone. Carl, Jack and many others made it work. What was the big deal with him, did he think she would try and change him or that she couldn't cope with this life? Well if he doesn't want any permanent ties, them forget him. No way am I letting myself in for that kind of heartache. He can just go to hell.

By the time the others had searched her out, she had decided she didn't need Ben. She would avoid being alone with him and treat their relationship as strictly business. He would never know how much she loved him. She had made it through a similar situation and she would make it through this one. When they returned to work she would work non-stop to finish this project and leave Mr. Macho Man to his life alone in his jungle.

It was hot and humid by the time they left the theater and the fun had gone out of the day and they were all ready to return to the hotel for a swim and relax before they met Mike for dinner.

Lonnie and Jack could feel the tension between Judy and Ben, but chose to ignore it. Judy looked out the window but didn't really see anything as they made the trip back to the hotel. It seemed to take forever.

Ben was taking care of the car as the others went inside. As they collected their keys the clerk informed them Mike was at the poolside and would they join him for a swim and drink.

Judy and Lonnie started for the elevator, "We will go on up honey, you can wait for Ben." Lonnie ushered Judy into the elevator. "Want to talk Judy?"

"No, not yet Lonnie, thanks." Judy's soft refusal made Lonny's heart ache.

"Don't keep it in honey. You will only hurt more."

They had arrived at Judy's door and as she turned the key to go in she could not hold back the tears any longer. Lonnie followed her into the room closing the door behind them. Judy was on the bed sobbing her heart out. Lonnie pulled her up and held her like she would Robbie or Becky.

"There, there, love just let it all out."

"Oh Lonnie, I was so sure Ben was beginning to feel the same as I do for him. I don't know yet if it is love, but he won't even give it a chance. He doesn't want any involvement he said. He just wants his work. I should have never stayed here. I knew from the start I was attracted to him. I kept telling myself I could handle it. I didn't flirt with him; I kept our relationship business. It was he who kissed me. I never tried to make him kiss me, it just happened. It is all his fault."

Lonnie let Judy ramble on until she had it all out and the crying had subsided. They were still sitting on the bed when they heard a soft knock on the door. Judy leaped off the bed and headed for the bathroom as Lonnie went to the door.

"It is only Jack." She yelled to Judy, then turned to Jack. "Honey, go on down. We will meet you later." Lonnie nodded her head to something Jack said as she closed the door.

The little interruption was what Judy needed. She washed her face and cooled off before returning to the other room.

"It was Jack. He went on down to the pool."

"Lonnie, I don't think I can go down. I'm afraid I will break down again and cry."

"No you won't. I won't let you. Anyway what if you do?"

"I can't let Ben know how much he hurt me. I will work day and night to get the project far enough along by Christmas so I won't have to come back after the holidays. If I get all the drawings finished, Ben, Mike and Carl can see it through. They won't need me."

"Is that what you want to do? Let someone else finish your project. You know you want to see it to the finish. You are one of the strongest women I have ever met. I know it's hard, but you can get through this, I know you can."

"I want to see it through to the finish, but I don't know."

"You can Judy. You didn't get this far in your career by quitting. I know you are hurt, but time will heal that hurt. Give it time Honey, don't make a decision you will regret later. Think it through before you make up your mind. Millie and I will be there for you."

"I feel better Lonnie, thanks for being here. I don't know what I would have done if you hadn't been here. I was even considering flying home, not even go back to the job. I know that was wrong, I just wasn't thinking straight. This is something I have worked for all my life and I don't intend to give it up. You're right and thanks."

"Come on let's get in your swimsuits. A good swim will relax you."

Judy and Lonnie went down to the pool to find the men swimming in the deep end of the pool. It was a large pool so Judy kept to herself while she enjoyed a long leisure swim. Mike was the first one to search her out. "Hi Punkin, did you have a good time?"

"I had an interesting time. How about you?"

"It was alright but not great." Mike looked at Judy. "Have you been crying? You look like you need a friend. You know you can come to me any time you need anything. I hope it was not Tony. I feel bad about deserting you, especially since my plans didn't work out."

"No it wasn't Tony. I am fine, I was just thinking about Lonnie, Jack and the kids leaving. Lonnie had been a real friend and I am going to miss her and the kids."

"You sure that's all it is."

"Mike, don't worry, I am ok."

After that it was easy. Judy latched onto the departure of Lonnie and her family as a crutch. She sincerely was going to miss them, but the hurt Ben had inflicted was much deeper.

They all dined at the Hotel together. They did not see Tony again nor did he call. Judy was a little concerned about Tony's feelings and hoped it would not have any effect on the business relationship. She was sure he was too mature to be vindictive.

Judy was sitting next to Mike sharing the days activities and the various things she found interesting. After dinner, they decided to walk off their meal. Mike, Judy, Jack and Lonnie started for the door when Ben excused himself saying he had some business to attend to.

They walked around the pool for a while. Jack and Lonnie soon gave up and decided to turn in. Judy and Mike said goodnight to them and walked on. They were both quiet for a while but Judy was sure Mike wanted to talk but wasn't quite ready or didn't know how to approach whatever he wanted to say.

He finally said, "Judy, let me ask you something."

"Sure Mike, what is it?"

"Do you think love can be enough if the woman must decide between the one she loves and her family?"

Judy thought for a few minutes and then said, "I don't know Mike, if she has to give up so much, she may eventually blame her lover for her loneliness and it would be very hard for a couple to survive on each other and not a family."

"I know, I feel that way too, but Adrian feels she wants to go against her family. They don't approve of me. I don't know what to do."

Judy and Mike walked and talked for a while, but could not solve Mike's problem and for sure Judy did not feel any better about hers, so they decided to call it a night.

As Judy entered her room, not bothering to turn on the light, she tossed her purse on the bed and opened the doors to let in the evening breeze. After undressing and turning back the covers, she was lying on the cool sheets, not able to sleep, when a familiar aroma drifting in on the night breeze. There was no mistaking the smell of Ben's pipe. He must be sitting on the veranda smoking. His way of relaxing he had told her. She would always remember him when she smelled that tobacco. It seems like years not months since she first arrived with all her clothes smelling like tobacco. With tears in her eyes she turned and buried her head in her pillow trying to shut it out. She must have succeeded because the next thing she knew she was scrambling to close out the down poor of rain and wind. She looked at her clock, it was just past two o'clock. She collapsed back on the bed and into an exhausting sleep.

Chapter 29

She woke the next morning early, anxious to be on her way, she showered and packed her suitcase. After calling to have it taken downstairs, she went down to the dining room for some much needed coffee.

As she entered the dining room the first person she saw was Ben. He was sitting at a table across the room by himself. At first she considered taking another table, but knowing how childish that would be, she started in the direction of his table. She had to work with him so she might just as well start dealing with it. Ben rose as Judy approached the table.

"Good Morning"

Judy took the chair across the table from Ben, "Good Morning," looking up at the waiter who had just walked up, she added, "coffee please, nothing else."

The waiter brought the coffee. The tension was unbearable; she wanted to start a conversation but could not think of anything to say.

"Is the plane ready?"

"Yes, I saw to it last night after dinner." Ben stood up; Judy turned to see Mike, Lonnie and Jack heading toward the table. Lonnie sat beside Judy and as she pulled her chair under her, she gave Judy a little pat on the knee under the table. It was a comforting jester, exactly what she needed. Lonnie was a great friend.

After breakfast they checked out to head home. Ben was driving, "Mike, we will let Judy fly the plane while you, Jack and I keep an eye out for anything unusual. We'll make a wide circle before landing Judy. We want to have a good look around before we land."

Jack looked at Lonny, who had turned pale, "What's up Ben?"

"May not be anything, Tony warned us to be on the alert. There may be some trouble. Some of the tribal Indians objects to our project. They feel we will destroy their rain forest. The government is trying to arrest them before it gets started, but as a precaution we want to keep an eye out. We'll make daily flights with the plane to keep watch and if we spot anything unusual we'll notify Tony. He will get some federal troops in to check it out."

It upset Lonnie. Jack was holding her hand and trying to reassure her, "The kids will be alright Honey. Don't worry. Carl and Millie will keep them safe, and if things stir up too much, I am sure Ben will fly the women and children out until it is over, right Ben?"

"You know we will Jack. In fact I don't think we will wait, I think it best if we take them out now for a few days and let Tony get things settled."

"I won't go, I want to stay with Jack. The children will be alright."

"I am not as concerned for the children as for the women Lonnie."

Judy had remained quiet during Ben and Lonny's discussion; "I won't leave unless the men all leave."

Everyone waited and wondered how Ben would handle the rebellious Judy. He said nothing for a few minutes. From where she was setting Judy could not see his expression, but she was sure he was furious. The side of his face she could see was red and he was so quiet she knew he was trying to keep his temper intact. After a few minutes he quietly said, "We'll see."

The hum of the plane and the quiet tension was taking its toll on Judy. She said, "I don't see how you can see anything except trees, it is so dense."

Without taking his eyes away from the window Mike said, "We are not looking for people or vehicles, it will be signs of camps. Smoke rising from the tree tops, birds taking flight all at once, things like that are what we're looking for."

"Smoke, mainly. It rises and since the only way to cook is open fire, there is usually some traces."

"I never thought of that." Judy said as she also started watching for the sign of smoke as well.

It was dark and they had landed. Everyone was out of the plane and she could see Millie bringing the children to meet Lonnie. She had secured everything on the plane and was getting ready to get down. As she stepped into the door, Ben reached for her.

She looked at him.

"Judy........." He lifted her down, stood for a minute looking in her eyes, then released his hold on her, turned and never finished whatever he started to say.

As Judy was collecting her luggage and packages the men were talking.

She heard Carl say; "Millie won't go."

As Judy got closer they lowered their voice so she could not make out what they were saying.

"How the hell can I make her leave if Millie and Lonnie stay?" Ben roared, "She had a better excuse for staying than anyone of them.

After all the fussing and cussing, Sharon, along with her baby, Becky and Robby were the only ones to fly out. Mike flew them out early Tuesday. Judy was in the work trailer when he radioed back; they had observed no sign of outsiders in the area.

The next few weeks everyone worked hard. Judy worked long hours herself out on the project most of the days and then working late into the night at her draft table. She made her word good, she stayed ahead of the men, barley, but enough. The plant was well under construction and the pipeline was almost ready to be connected. Torrential rains had slowed them from time to time, but when it rained, Judy had Carl put all the men to work inside putting finishing touches on the home. Not a minute was wasted. She drove the men as hard as she drove herself. Millie and Lonnie watched her driving herself and the men to point of breaking but said nothing. Judy stayed so busy she had no time to think. Her heart ached and at night, exhausted, she still cried herself to sleep.

Chapter 30

Almost every weekend Judy flew Millie and Lonnie to Manaus to see the children. Mike took a turn occasionally but Judy was sure it was their way of protecting the women as much as they could. "Three stubborn women," Carl had said one day when they were all together heading out to the plane.

It was one of those early Monday morning flights the three women were returning when Judy spotted smoke as they approached the project. "I'll circle, you two try and see what is going on and if you can tell if there is trouble."

She circled high so she would not draw attention.

"They have our men on the pipeline road," Lonnie yelled. "Judy what are we going to do?"

Judy was already on the radio to Tony. She had seen the danger.

"Let me circle again and see for myself the situation." All the time she was circling she was on the radio giving information to the federal office. Judy tilted the little plane and made a wide sweep. She could see what had happened. Most of the men were sealed off on the connecting road.

The workers were at the plant end, so she saw only a few guarding the end leading to the housing. If they could scare them off, we could get weapons to our men and possibly they could hold off until the federal troops arrived. Judy was planning in her mind what to do as she headed away from the site so they would think she flew back to the city. She made a wide circle and came in just above the trees and hoped she fooled them. She landed and was out of the plane in seconds. Tony was in the office when she radioed. Maybe he would get things going quickly.

"Thank God some of the men are here." Millie observed.

As they got out of the plane, four men came running to them.

"We heard shooting but didn't know whether to stay here or go help," One of them said, "it just started."

"Go load all the weapons and ammunition you can find in the jeep," Judy took command.

"Lonnie, Millie if you can shoot we need all the guns we can get. If you don't want to go I'll understand. Just stay inside."

"We're with you 'Kiddo'," Millie said as Lonnie nodded her head.

The men came back with enough firearms to put up a healthy fight. Judy slung a rifle over her shoulder and checked a second one to make sure it was loaded. The others did the same. The men had filled the jeep with everything they could find in record time and then Judy had some of them climb on the truck . "Millie you drive the truck,

Lonnie, you drive the jeep. Stay here until you hear up firing, then you two drive like hell follow us as close as you can through that opening to the road and don't stop until you see our men. Can you do it?"

Lonnie nodded her head without speaking, Judy knew she was scared. They all were.

Judy took a deep breath, "We must clear this end so we don't have any of them behind us. When we get close, I will fire the first shot, when you hear my shot open fire and keep firing. We want them to think they have an army after them. Don't worry about hitting anything, just keep firing, we want to clear the opening to let Lonnie and Millie through to the men then Millie you and Lonnie turn around and get out of there.

Lonnie, stayed back a little with the jeep engine running, once we start firing watch for my signal then drive like the devil is after you, we have to get guns to the men get them away from those guards. Hopefully we can catch them off guard long enough for the men to get the guns. We'll have to keep the opening clear until all the men are out. Remember Lonnie wait for me to signal. Everyone ready?"

They all nodded.

Judy got in a truck, Millie climbed in hers, and they drove until they came to the first house. Judy got out leaving the door open so as not to make a noise. She and the men started moving forward in all directions, using the homes as cover, they moved closer. When in position she fired her first shot at the feet of two of the men, spitting gravel over them. Guns exploded from all over the area and as Judy suspected the surprise and amount of firing, the men took off in the opposite direction as fast as they could run.

As she headed for her truck she stepped out and motioned for Lonnie to go, and go she did.

She shot past Judy driving, Judy guessed, fifty miles an hour and right behind her was Millie in the other truck. So much for following me. I will be lucky if I catch up with them before they reach the men. Thank god there was someone in with both them. Lonny will be sore for weeks from that ride Judy thought.

Judy jumped in the open door of the truck she had left running and took off as fast as she could to catch up. The men were following in the dust the jeep stirred up. Some of the men had positioned themselves on second floor of the guesthouse, which still had open sides. One of Carl's men she noticed had climbed on the roof of one of the houses across from the guesthouse. They would keep the opening clear for their return She waved as he looked around. It didn't take long before gunfire was heard. She knew Lonnie had accomplished her mission so she stopped and waited. She did not want any of them regrouping at the opening to the camp.

It seemed like a long time before she saw the men coming down the road, but it was only minutes. Judy looked anxiously in the direction they were coming from for sight of Ben. She wondered how long they had been trapped and if any had been shot. All the men were her concern but one in particular was foremost in her mind as the little convoy came into sight. Lonnie leading, still driving the jeep and

Jack was sitting beside her. His hand was wrapped in a make shift bandage. Bloody, but obviously not too bad. Loaded in the back of the jeep were several other men hanging their feet over the side for room. She did not see Ben. Next was the large open bed truck. All the men were standing and sitting on the back. It was so crowded; she could not make out who all was there. Mike drove and Carl was in the passenger side with Millie sandwiched between the two big men. She forgot about Millie. She must have been the one driving the truck.. Lord, she must have been crazy to plan such a stunt. She could have gotten everyone killed.

They came to a halt where Judy was positioned as lookout. Some of the men got out to take over for her. One said I'll drive if you want. She looked down and slipped out of the big truck seat, as she thanked the men , she saw Ben lying on the back with men sitting on both sides of him.

She ran to the truck "How bad is he hurt, was he shot?"

Her face was white with fear as Carl came around the truck and put his arm around her. "Honey, it's ok, the bullet went through his leg. It's good you got us out though. Infection sets in fast down here. Tore the skin up pretty bad. It hit just above the knee. Didn't hit a bone but he lost a lot of blood and we need to get it cleaned right away.

You go with him, I will take over and make sure they don't come down that road. Millie said you had contacted Tony. Did you get an answer before landing?"

Mike came up as they were talking. "Thanks Judy, great job. You sure used your head. Did you hear from Tony?"

"Not really, I talked to him briefly and he said leave everything to him. He ordered me back to Manaus but I pretended I had shut the radio down. Don't give me away."

The men all laughed and Mike shook his head. "Your secret is safe with us little lady, " one of the workers was saying, "we were in a real mess. The boss wounded with no medicine to treat his wound. We were in a real trap. No telling when help would come. After today we will follow you to hell and back." They all laughed.

"Let's just hope it isn't necessary Luke, but thanks for the confidence."

"Mike make sure anyone with scratches or wounds get them taken care of. We don't need infections setting in."

"Will do Punkin', you go on with the truck, Carl and I will run it from here. If you hear shots, everyone come running with loaded guns."

"Thanks guys, I'm glad everyone is safe and hope help is not far away."

Chapter 31

Help did come late that afternoon. A cargo plane landed with several federal troops. They took off through the jungle in search of the attackers. Judy had been helping Millie and Lonnie with the men. All the scratches and wounds had been cleaned good and bandaged. The attack had been early that morning while the men were on their way to the plant. That is why they were all together. Having only two guns with them, Ben had tried to talk to their leader. That is when he was shot. The men all took cover and fired a few shots so the attackers pulled back, either waiting for reinforcements or until dark, they had sealed off the road back to the camp. It didn't appear to be a big group, nor were they very well organized. Either way it was just as well the ladies had made their daring rescue.

Ben commented on how well she handled the situation, but also stressed how upset he was that she acted before she had Tony's help. It was all she could do to keep from touching him, or someway reach out to him. She longed for the comfort of his arms around her but instead she muttered a thank you and walked away to help Millie.

Judy had cleaned up and was sitting on the porch. Ben was lying on a cot they had brought out. She had seen him watching her from time to time, while she worked on the other men. She turned to look at him, their eyes met.

"Judy, come here, please."

She got up and slowly walked over to the cot where he was laying. "Do you need something Ben?"

"Yes, I need something." His voice was barely a whisper.

She stared in wonderment, waiting to hear what he needed.

He reached for her hand and pulled gently, "I need you Judy. I want to hold you and kiss you so I know you are ok."

"Ben." She gave in to the gentle tug of his hand as she sat on the edge of the cot. He let go of her hand as he reached for the back of her neck. Her whole world turned over as his lips met hers. She kissed him as tears started to flow.

"Ben…Ben…" as she buried her face in the hollow of his neck to hide the tears.

"Judy don't cry. It's alright now." Ben comforted her and the shock of all the day's happenings overtook Judy.

"Lord, what a mess I have made of things. I did not want this to happen. From the first day you arrived, you got under my skin. You and your stubborn ways have proved me wrong all the way. You are one of the best architects I have ever worked with. You stood up to the heat, the working conditions as well as any of us. You work as hard as any man and now you lead an army of men and women to chase off a band of gorillas. I had the nerve to say you could not handle a life like this."

He pushed her up slightly so he could look into her eyes. He gently brushed away each tear with his thumbs as he held her face between his big callused hands.

"What are we going to do my darling Judy?" All I have been thinking of is what would have happened if you had been captured by those men. They would put you through hell before you could kill yourself to be free of their torture."

He pulled her hard against him, "Promise me you will go to Manaus and stay until this is settled. You can work out of Tony's office. "Promise me, Judy!"

"Alright Ben, but they better get those........" She held back the word she wanted to say as Ben once again pulled her to him, laughing at her.

Several men along with Millie and Lonnie were sitting on the porch talking. Judy and Ben were oblivious to their surroundings, until one of the men spoke louder than usual.

"You know Carl, I understand why Ben warned us to stay away from Judy when she first came down here to work. He wanted her for himself."

Ben smiled up at Judy, who was still sitting beside him on the little cot. "You know, I am in for some real harassing, rightly so too. I warned the men when you first arrive they were to treat you with respect and keep their distance."

"You're right 'Shorty,' Carl was saying, "He had always been one to spot the best before the rest of us. He believes in cutting out competition before it gets a foot in the door."

"Don't know but what he deserves what he is getting. I think he might have met his match when it comes to bossing and ordering around. That little lady came out of that plane spitting orders to us and we were off doing her bidding before we even knew what for. Yes, he met his match." They all laughed.

Judy's face was pink and flushed. "I think I better go get your pipe and some tobacco. You are going to need something to keep you calm and cool. You're right, they will not let you off easy."

Judy took a friendly punch at Carl's shoulder as she passed him on the way to the steps off the porch. They were laughing and having a good time. Judy knew they would all get in on it before it was over. She would just as soon not hear it.

The sun was setting and a cool breeze blew her hair away from her face. It had grown so much since she came down here. The climate must make hair grow also, she thought as she lifted it off her damp neck.

Mike came running after her; "I'll walk with you." He carried a rifle slung over his shoulder; it brought her back to reality.

"It isn't over is it Mike?"

"Not by a long shot 'Punkin'. You and the other ladies are leaving here at dawn. None of us could live with ourselves if one of you were captured. They use the women and kill them when they move on Judy. It is not anything to take lightly. I had a long talk with Tony, he was really upset when you didn't return to Manaus. He said he was sure you still had the radio on. He respects you for your work and how you conduct yourself professionally, and if he cannot see you socially, he at least wants to be considered a friend. He said he didn't realize until your visit that Ben was also attracted to you. He said to tell you he did not want to jeopardize two good friendships. He has a great respect for the both of you. That goes for all of the men and me as well, Judy. We all could see it coming. We also knew Ben would fight it to Hell and back, but we had our bets on you. We wanted you to win and I think you have. I am just sorry it wasn't me, but I mean what I say, you are leaving here in the morning and you won't come back until Tony feels it is safe."

Judy was crying again. "Mike I know it was a dangerous thing to do. I was so scared for all of you. They looked to me for guidance and with all of you captured, I figured I was the only one in charge. I know I was lucky there was only a few men on this end. I don't know what I would have done if they had not run."

The seriousness of the situation was beginning to sink in for Judy; and now that she was relaxing, she was feeling the effect of it.

It is over for now, but at first light, I am flying you, Millie and Lonnie out of here even if I have to tie you in the plane. Ben and Carl will have my hide if I don't. I am more afraid of them than you."

As they entered their trailer, "Now what was so important, we had to make a trip over here?"

Judy smiled as she went over and picked up Ben's pipe and tobacco. Mike shook his head and laughed, "might as well pack a bag while you are here. We are all staying together tonight. Not much sleep for anyone I'm afraid. We will take some of our blankets and pillows, we can use them on the floor to sleep on."

They didn't take long to get things together and return to were the others were. Judy did not want to be alone. Not after what Ben and Mike had said why they were so worried.

Chapter 32

Judy had positioned herself in a chair next to Ben's cot. She was holding his hand as they both tried to sleep. Ben was restless and a little feverish, but as the night turned to morning Judy could tell his fever was gone. He was sleeping peacefully, more than she could say for herself. She had been awake most of the night, thinking about her situation with Ben. Did Ben love her enough to marry her and let her work with him or would he let her go when the job was finished? She loved him and would do anything to be with him, but if he didn't want marriage, she would not settle for an affair. When the project was finished, would he just let her go? Before yesterday, she had made up her mind to go home and forget Ben, now she didn't know what to do.

As the sky showed signs of day-bread, Mike rousted everyone. Judy let go of Ben's hand as she got up out of her chair. Stiff from spending the night in a chair, she stretched and twisted to work out the kinks.

Ben raised up and put his feet on the floor. He bent forward with his head down. "I guess I lost some blood, my head is swimming a little. Give me a minute and I'll walk down to the plane with you."

"You have a bad wound. You should have a doctor check it out."

"I'm fine. Just give me a minute."

"Sit still, I'll get us some coffee."

They had their coffee in their hand but Mike was anxious to leave. He said they could eat at the hotel. It had rained most of the night and was still raining a little. It was muddy and Judy knew in normal circumstances, Mike would not take the plane up, it was going to be a rough flight. They were all in except Judy. Ben held her for a few minutes. He finally eased his hold and kissed he softly on the tip of her nose.

"Get aboard and don't look back."

He lifted her in the plane and slammed the door shut. Mike had the plane moving away from them as the door closed Millie reached over and squeezed her shoulder. "They'll be alright Honey. Tony will clear things up and we will be back in no time."

They took off and Mike made a wide sweep of the area, with the rain it was not likely they would see anything. Judy radioed back that everything looked ok as they headed for Manaus.

Mike looked over at her, "What is bothering you Punkin? You are too quiet."

Judy turned to Mike, her eyes sparkled from unshed tears, "Mike be honest with me when I ask you something. I have to know."

"I'll try, what's up?"

She glanced around, Millie and Lonnie appeared to be sleeping.

"Mike you know Ben and I have......, well we have found we have a mutual attraction. It has not gone beyond that. When we were in town that weekend, he told me he did not want to get involved and that his job was too important to him. So I have been working by buns off to finish this job to the point when we go home for the holidays, I planned on not returning. It will be far enough along that you and he can see it through and I will leave him to his job and his work without an involvement."

Judy sat a few minutes before continuing. Mike waited. "The incident yesterday and the emotions of it all caused the feeling to surface again. I don't know if Ben has changed his mind or if I should pack it in and go home like I planned so he can get on with his life. Do you and he want things to stay the same? I don't know what to do,"

Judy fell silent; Mike didn't answer for a few minutes. He made a half laugh and half-dejected sound, "Why did you have to fall for that big lug? Tony or I either one would give up the world for you, job be dam."

"Mike, I'm sorry, I didn't know. I like you. You are so easy to talk to, but I guess we don't always do what's right do we?"

Mike reached across and ran his finger down her cheek in a caress. "I knew from the first day there was a spark between you and Ben. I wondered how long it would take the two of you to discover it. Everyone knew and we were all happy about it. Ben is a great guy and we were all hoping you would crack that tough shield he puts up, but Punkin, I can't say. Ben and I have worked together for almost ten years, and he never has been one to talk things out. He is a loaner. I am afraid you are on your own. He keeps things to himself, always has. I can tell you one thing, whatever he sets his mind to do, he always did it, until you came along.

He was going to contact Stewart to have you transferred back home, but he didn't, he warned everyone to keep their distance, he didn't, he wanted everyone to fly out at the first sign of danger, he didn't make you go. He may want you enough to change his ways on this also. I can't say. I do know since you came back from that weekend in town he has been like a bear with a sore tooth. The men and I have avoided him like a plague. He was so worried you would not see the fighting and land right in the middle of things. We were afraid some of you would be captured. We kept a smoke fire going so you could see there was trouble and return to Manaus. He never dreamed you would try a rescue. The fool got shot trying to talk to those people before your plane arrived. He was afraid you would get captured. I don't know what else I can say. You may have to do some persuading if you want him bad enough. The old boy won't give up his bachelor life without a fight. I do know that. The question you have to ask yourself is, do you want him bad enough and is he worth it?"

Mike wasn't much help. She was no closer to figuring out her problem than she was when she woke up this morning.

"We're ready to land," Mike was saying, "I won't stay. I'll refuel, grab a bite to eat and get back as soon as I can. They may need the plane. We will stay in touch."

Mike was busy with the radio and landing the plane so the conversation was over.

They waved goodbye to Mike as they headed for a taxi. "I wonder how long we will have to be in town?" Millie did not like city living and would not stay any longer than necessary. She had made the jungle her home for over fifteen years, Judy was thinking, could I do that? Would it satisfy my need for a home and family, was it worth it to be with Ben? That was what Mike asked, "Do you want him enough to fight for him?" There were so many questions going around in her head as the taxi rushed through the morning traffic to the hotel.

"Judy, honey, we won't be in town long. You'll see. Tony will get those guerillas and lock them up. Then we can go back."

"I hope so Millie."

CHAPTER 33

The hotel had some family bungalows which Tony had acquired for the family visits so that is where they were to be living for the next few days or weeks for however long it took before they could return to the construction site.

Judy contacted the home office as soon as they got settled in at the hotel. She gave them a report on all that had happened, leaving out as much as she could to minimize the danger. She didn't need Mr. Hardell insisting on her returning home at this time. There were questions and Judy answered them as best she could. The main thing she wanted them to know was that everyone was ok. She stressed there was a few injuries, the worst was the bullet wound on Ben's leg, which she assured them had passed though some flesh, missing bone completely and that he was walking around and doing fine. She also informed them there was no damage to the project and our local federal contact was already at the construction site with troops. They expected to have control very soon.

Tony made arrangements for Judy to work at his office where she had access to the radio and could stay in contact with the men at the project. She was glad she had something to fill her days. Time dragged by. It had been over a week and things were still not settled. It had rained almost every day and the men could hardly get through the mud to the plant. Tony's men found no trace of the attackers and figured with the rain they had given up the fight. There were still guards around the project and the women were not allowed to return, not even Judy, who kept insisting she needed to be there.

It was the first week of November when Ben sent word they were going to shut down for the holidays. The men would be flown over and everyone was to be ready for the trip home by the weekend. The company plane would be there and pick up everyone. A few men were staying behind with Mike and Ben. Carl, Jack and David were coming so they could go with their wives.

Judy received word through Carl that she was to go home on the plane with the families. He gave her a note from Ben.

It read: "We are closing down for the holidays, due to all the rain. Mike and I will be a while. You go home with the others. Your work is close to completion so you don't need to return after the break, Mike and I can finish up. We will have the plant connected and running by the end of January. Record time, and a great job. I am sure Stewart will be pleased. "

He had just signed, Ben. No thank you, no see you or no anything for that matter, just 'Ben.'

After Judy read the note, she then reread it. She was not hurt, she was angry. "Not come back my ass. I will be back Mr. High and Mighty, and I'll tell you when my part of the project is completed. You don't make decisions for me. I have never left an unfinished job and I won't start with this one. Oh yes, I'll be back, you can bet on it."

Chapter 34

The end of the week came fast, but everyone was ready and waiting for the plane. Saturday came and they were loaded, ready for takeoff by nine that morning. Judy sat with Millie and Carl and they discussed their plans for the next few weeks. Judy invited them to her parent's house for Christmas since they did not have family. They agreed, if it was ok with her parents, they would love to spend the holiday with her. Carl and Judy were expected to be in the office the first part of the week to give reports to Mr. Hardell before Judy could leave for home.

Judy and Carl were discussing how much had been accomplished while she was away. "I wish I could have made a trip to see everything before I left."

Carl said, "As soon as the plane took off that day after the attack, Ben and Mike started working the men from sun up to sun down, seven days a week. It wouldn't surprise me if Ben didn't have the plant ready to power up before he and Mike leave. The homes and guest house are finished and as soon as the sewer can be hooked up, they will let the workers move in."

He said Tony had been there the whole time as well. "He swings a lot of weight. He and Mike have become good friends. Ben's leg is giving him a little trouble, it should have had stitches."

Seeing her concern, he added, "Don't you worry little lady, he will be alright. Tony will insist they get out of there pretty soon. They can't do much as it is."

Judy and Carl finally ran out of anything to talk about and Carl dozed off. Judy closed her eyes but sleep was not easy coming for her. She could not keep Ben out of her thoughts. Her concern for his health and safety were ever present.

They landed in New York to a freezing cold rain. No one was dressed for it and the cold wind was biting into her tropical skin. It was amazing how quickly your body adjusted to its surroundings. Judy remembered the breathtaking heat she had stepped into over eight months ago and thought she would never get use to it, now she was in a freezing New York thinking the same thing about the cold.

Monday morning, Carl, Millie and Judy went in to the Head office. They were greeted warmly by everyone and all the staff was eager to hear firsthand about their encounter with the gorillas. Carl was in his glory telling the story and making Judy out a war hero.

Judy was a little embarrassed and tried in vain to stop him. Millie touched her arm, "Honey, let him be. He is in his glory. That man thinks you're about the world's best. Listen to him, now he's making me out to be a gun touting wife. I don't think I hit anything except maybe the treetops, I was so scared."

"We did take quite a chance Millie. I would not be so impetuous next time."

"That's good to hear." They both jumped at the sound of the masculine voice behind them. "I was going to bring up that very thing, but I see it isn't necessary." Mr. Hardell reached out his hand, "Welcome home."

"Thank you Mr. Hardell. No, it is not necessary. I do understand more now and I will be more cautious in the future."

He joined in with the office staff and their well wishes for a few minutes and them invited Carl and Judy into his office for a first hand report on the project.

When they were ready to leave, Judy ask, "Mr. Hardell, "may I have a word alone with you?"

She looked at Carl; "It's personal. I need to talk to him alone for a few minutes. I will be only a minute."

Carl understood, "I'll be out side with Millie, take your time."

Judy sat back down, trying to decide how to start.

"You have a problem?"

Judy looked at her hands in her lap, "Yes I do. I have a special request, but before I make it, I think you deserve an explanation or at least some background so you will know why I am doing it."

"Sounds fair, go ahead."

It was almost an hour before Judy and Mr. Hardell came out of his office. Carl and Millie were waiting.

"Carl, this is some lady I hired. Tell me, would you work for her on another job in the field?"

"You dam right I would. She is one of the best bosses I have ever had, Mike and Ben included. She worked alongside us and kept the project moving without delays. She can handle men and she is good at design. Never had to wait for material and supplies. Of course it helped to have the Brazilian representative in her back pocket," he laughed as he concluded.

"Thanks Carl, that tells me all I need to know." He was laughing as he went down the hall to his office.

"What was that all about Judy?"

"You'll see Carl, you'll see." Judy picked up her coat; "Come on lets go Christmas shopping."

Judy was happy to see her family. She had been lax in her letter writing so she had a great deal of catching up to do. Her mother spoiled her with breakfast in bed and cooked her favorite meals, they shopped for new clothes, but it was her talks she enjoyed the most. They always discussed everything openly, so it was only natural her problem with Ben came up.

"I thought he loved me, but then I get the impression from his last message he still wants to forget everything."

She had broke down and cried while she was telling her story. Her mother comforted her, but her father just sat and waited for it all to come out before he spoke.

"Well Love, it looks like you have two ways to go. You cannot go back, just throw your hands up and say it's over and be done with it or, you can go back and see the finish of the project and confront your young man for a decision. I have watched you from the time you were born Honey, you have always bit off a mouthful, but you never spit it out. You have never been one to quit or give up, but if you feel that is what you want, then that's all right too. We love you, we will support you whatever your decision."

"I love you both," Judy said as she got up and hugged them.

"I'm going back and I have Mr. Hardell's permission to go back and finish the job. I also have a plan that will push my undecided friend off the fence, one way or the other. I may need a lot of love and support if he jumps the wrong way, but I can't leave it like this."

Her Mother looked worried as her father smiled and nodded his head. Judy knew she was taking a chance but she had to know for sure whether Ben loved her enough to give up his single way of life for one with her. The uncertainty was worse than the possibility of loosing him completely. She would deal with it if it came to that, but she had made her decision, she was going back.

CHAPTER 35

The holidays were over. Millie and Carl had come for Christmas and with Judy's help, her mother had persuaded them to stay the rest of the time with them. Millie and her mother got along so well. Millie said it was hard to say good-by when the time came to go back to New York.

It was the middle of January when Judy, Millie, Carl and most of the crew headed back to Brazil. Ben and Mike would be coming later with the supplies and equipment. Judy had not seen any of them since they left in November. Tony flew them over to the site. He had cleared the area of all resistance and the homes were almost all occupied. Judy took a room in the new guesthouse rather than the trailer with Ben and Mike. The plant was running and everything seemed to be operating fine, Ben must have stayed most of the time to get it finished.

"Looks like we can move on Kiddo!" Wonder what the new assignment is going to be?" Carl and Judy were driving back from inspecting everything.

"Millie will have some lunch for us while we wait for Ben and Mike."

They had just finished their lunch when they heard the plane. Judy chose to wait with Millie while Carl went to meet them with the jeep. Judy got up and started clearing the table and washing up to have something to do. She didn't know how Ben would react to her being there.

Millie just watched and said nothing. The men were coming in the door, Judy was still at the sink with her back to the door. She hadn't turned around, but she knew Ben was there before he spoke. He threw two large packs on the table as he spoke.

"It seems we have some decisions to make before we start our new assignments."

Mike said, "We have two major jobs at the same time and Stew wants us to divide into two teams now that Judy has proved herself. She requested to work in the field for another three to five years and he gave his permission. However, he feels one of us with more experience should work with her. He left it up to us on how we wanted to divide up."

"He ask me when I was home if I would work with Judy again. I said I would work with her anytime, anywhere," Carl spoke with certainty.

"He knows Judy and I have a good friendship. I will be glad to work with you Judy."

Judy was leaning against the sink for support, waiting for Ben's answer. Ben was looking at her; "I will let you know my decision after I have had a talk to Judy."

At least he didn't say go to hell. Judy's hopes rose a little as she went over to the table where the others were looking over the projects.

Only one required design work, the other one would use plans from a previous job. They were all gathered around the table discussing the jobs when Judy felt a touch on her arm. She turned as Ben indicated with a nod of his head; he wanted her to go outside. They moved in the direction of the door without a word. The little group at the table trying to appear disinterested let them go without notice.

Judy's heart was beating so fast she could hardly breath. They walked to the jeep and Ben lifted her in. He stood for a moment holding her attention with his eyes, waiting for her to say something. Neither said a word. Ben finally went around to the driver seat and started the engine. Judy wondered where they were going. Did he want to show her the finished work? She just waited as he sped along in the jeep, past the homes and as they came to the road to the plant, instead of turning towards the river he turned towards the swimming area where they had spent so many afternoons. It was cool this time of the year and the trees and vines were heavy from the long rains.

They arrived at the pool area and Ben pulled the jeep to a stop. As he came around, she waited for him to help her down. He smiled as he took hold of her waist and lifted her down slowly, "Let's walk a ways."

Ben was holding her hand and as they reached the big old tree they used to dive off of, he turned her around and pulled her to him. He moaned as though he was in pain as his lips closed over hers. It was like a release of floodwater. Judy could not get enough of him. She was clinging to him as they sank to the ground, He devoured her with kisses.

Ben's lips left hers to travel a sensuous road with kisses to first her ear them down her neck leaving trails of fire wherever his lips touched. Her blouse had come open and as his kisses approached her already aroused breast, her body on its own volition arched in response to the pleasure she felt. Her bra was pushed aside and the release made it possible for Ben to continue his trail of fire to first one breast then the other. Judy arching and pulling him to her, wanting more. They were frantic with desire for each other.

Ben stopped and pulled away slightly, trying to gain control of his emotions he started planting light kisses as his mouth traveled the same trail in reverse, moaned her name as his mouth once again covered hers.

"Judy, we have to talk. I can't think right now, let alone talk rationally. I missed you so much. I worked like hell trying to get you out of my system, but if you had not come back I would have come after you. Stew told us you came down on the first flight. I thought that dam plane I was on would never get to Brazil, and the closer we got the slower it seemed to fly." He laughed, "Mike said for his sake he hoped you were in Manaus waiting for us."

"We came over with Tony, leaving the plane for you and Mike. I wanted to be here when I talked to you."

Judy sat up, while Ben lay on the grass next to her. "I love you Ben. I think I did from the very first week we met, but I have shielded myself for so long against getting emotionally involved on a job. I wanted to be accepted on my work alone. I wouldn't admit even to myself that I loved you. Not until you were trapped by those men. I didn't care what happened to me, I had to get to you and get you out. I know it was a stupid thing to do and I won't do that again."

Ben took her in his arms again and pulled her down so her head was lying on his chest. She could hear his heart pounding. He was holding her so tight she could hardly breath.

"I think that is when I came to terms with my feelings as well. But after you left, I felt it was not fair to expose you to such dangers and decided I would try and forget. I worked like hell and I couldn't get you out of my mind. I would wake up at night, thinking of the times I held you in my arms. It was hopeless. As time passes, I missed you more rather than less. Mike had one hell of a time putting up with me."

"Poor Mike, he is so good. He told me about his dream and how her family won't accept him."

Ben laughed, "Not to worry my pet, we will probably be attending one of the biggest weddings in Brazil next year. Tony, it seems, knows her family and put in a good word for our friend and things are progressing very well."

"We better get back, it's getting dark and the others will be anxious to see if your little scheme worked. I knew when I talked to Stewart that you were telling me you would work in the field and that I could not use that as an excuse. I also knew marriage was the only way I could have you. You will marry me won't you?"

"Yes, I'll marry you."

"We will work in the field a few more years, but like Jack and Lonnie, when the kids are near school age we will settle down in a real home."

"The kids, just how many do you want?"

"Dozens," he said, as he rolled over with her, pinning her to the ground. Under the century old tree, as the abundant waterfall cascaded over the rocks into the pool. Judy said yes to Ben's lifetime offer.

The End